It felt as if they had been made for one another, as if they fitted like two halves of a whole.

They hesitated between gentle and pure need and she gave a small snuffle of a plea she might be embarrassed about later, then snuggled even closer to his mighty body without making any of the maidenly protests she ought to if she was a truly virtuous woman.

Darius shifted his stance so they could fit closer together and little flashes of lightning seemed to spark inside her everywhere they touched—all over her, and all over him fire was ready to break out—and his mouth slanted and she opened hers hungrily. Intimacy she had never even let herself dream of until now flared to life between them and it felt utterly glorious. She had good instincts, she decided foggily as their mouths clung hotly and played like lovers'. No, they *were* lovers.

Never mind the details; never mind the denial she felt somewhere in him beyond all this heat and light and did not want to think about. Right now, they were lovers. The everyday Fliss had melted away and a new one stood in her place, and she was brazen.

Author Note

Welcome to the first of my new Yelverton trilogy about the children of a country vicar and his well-connected wife. It sounds like a wonderful windfall for a Regency gentleman and former soldier to inherit a fine old house and run-down estate from his mother's uncle, but what if it needed a fortune spent on it and he did not have one? Thinking about his dilemma sparked this book off. While writing about Darius Yelverton's struggle with his demons and his inconvenient attraction to the apparently penniless Miss Felicity Grantham, I got very fond of the Yelvertons and could not bring myself to say goodbye to them, so Darius's two sisters are next and I do hope you will come with me on that adventure, as well.

Thank you for being my lovely readers. Without you an author is nothing. I also want to thank my wonderful and very patient editor, Julia Williams, for all her help and understanding while we try to make the best book we can out of my wild ideas. You are the reason we both do what we do. Thank you, Julia; you are a star, and I would like to dedicate this book to you.

ELIZABETH BEACON

——

Marrying for Love
or Money?

HISTORICAL™

ISBN-13: 978-1-335-50537-8

Marrying for Love or Money?

Copyright © 2020 by Elizabeth Beacon

All rights reserved. No part of this book may be used or reproduced in
any manner whatsoever without written permission except in the case of
brief quotations embodied in critical articles and reviews.

This is a work of fiction. Names, characters, places and incidents
are either the product of the author's imagination or are used fictitiously.
Any resemblance to actual persons, living or dead, businesses,
companies, events or locales is entirely coincidental.

This edition published by arrangement with Harlequin Books S.A.

For questions and comments about the quality of this book,
please contact us at CustomerService@Harlequin.com.

Harlequin Enterprises ULC
22 Adelaide St. West, 40th Floor
Toronto, Ontario M5H 4E3, Canada
www.Harlequin.com

Printed in U.S.A.

Elizabeth Beacon has a passion for history and storytelling and, with the English West Country on her doorstep, never lacks a glorious setting for her books. Elizabeth tried horticulture, higher education as a mature student, briefly taught English and worked in an office before finally turning her daydreams about dashing piratical heroes and their stubborn and independent heroines into her dream job: writing Regency romances for Harlequin Historical.

Books by Elizabeth Beacon

Harlequin Historical

A Rake to the Rescue
The Duchess's Secret
Marrying for Love or Money?

The Alstone Family

A Less Than Perfect Lady
Rebellious Rake, Innocent Governess
One Final Season
A Most Unladylike Adventure
A Wedding for the Scandalous Heiress

A Year of Scandal

The Viscount's Frozen Heart
The Marquis's Awakening
Lord Laughraine's Summer Promise
Redemption of the Rake
The Winterley Scandal
The Governess Heiress

Visit the Author Profile page
at Harlequin.com for more titles.

Chapter One

Fliss tried to ignore the panicky feeling that she might never find her friend's dog again in this wild wood. Perhaps she should go back to Miss Donne's house and admit she had lost it, but since she was lost herself she might as well keep looking.

She scurried down an unkempt path and wished she had insisted on walking alone this morning, despite her former governess's protests. And she was no nearer to working out what to do next either.

The whole country was rejoicing and she felt out of step as she worried her way around this dratted wood. Napoleon had abdicated two months ago and the war that gripped Europe for most of her life was over. She was alive on a fine June day, had good friends and a profession she managed to enjoy until her latest employment ended and the sun was very definitely shining. Oh, and she was rich, thanks to her late godmother's astonishing bequest of thirty thousand pounds. She had a very eligible offer to consider while she took a holiday with Miss Donne and there was still time to find the wretched animal before they were truly missed.

Then she remembered the latest tear-blotched letter from Juno Defford and frowned despite all those reasons to be cheerful. Her former pupil dreaded crowds of strangers and noisy, stuffy rooms, but Juno's grandmother, the Dowager Viscountess Stratford, had ignored the girl's fears and Fliss's protests and insisted Juno make her debut in polite society while the bloom of youth was still on her. It had been a total disaster. The poor girl was miserable and lonely, despite London being *en fête* for the victorious Allied Sovereigns' visit to celebrate peace. But Juno was in London and Fliss was here and she still had a dog to find, so she must worry about her former pupil later.

'Luna,' she called without much hope of being listened to. 'Lu-n-a!' she bellowed, although the sharp little creature was even less likely to come if she heard anger in her voice. '*Wretched* animal,' she muttered darkly.

There, she was right, she *had* heard a distant and excited yip, yip almost in reply when she called last time and she impulsively plunged into this wild and ill-kept wood after her. Luna even sounded a little closer this time; not as if she meant to come when she was called, but nearby was a lot better than over the hills and far away. Fliss broke into a trot, then a run when Luna's surprisingly deep bark sounded ever more excited and closer than ever. She almost dared hope the little dog was tired of hide and seek and might come to her if she managed to get closer before she called her again. She tried to judge how long ago they had left Broadley Town from the length of shadows the trees were casting now. Which meant she was not looking where she was going when she stumbled over an exposed tree root. Flailing her arms to regain her balance, she knew it was too late to avoid the puddle of mud at the foot of the tree even as she pitched forward with a jarring thump and hit the ground so hard the breath whooshed out of her with a startled 'Oomph'.

Sprawled headlong in the surprisingly cold puddle that was still here even in midsummer, thanks to the lie of the land and the dark shadow cast by the mighty oak, her soft landing felt like a mixed blessing. Mud was soaking through her light summer gown until she felt as if she might as well have bathed naked in the awful stuff. She wrinkled her nose and fought a strong urge to gag at the stench of stagnant slime. Now she was filthy; lost and still without her friend's beloved pet.

Blinking back tears of shock and frustration, she gasped for air and made herself assess the damage to her limbs and body before she got cross about ruining every single garment she had on and still having to find her way back to Broadley and Miss Donne's house in this sorry state. Apart from stinging knees, one or two bruises and bruised and grazed hands where she had tried to save herself as she hit the ground it could be a lot worse, she supposed philosophically. She was disgustingly dirty and sore, but at least nothing felt broken or sprained and she did not appear to be bleeding.

A couple of choice phrases were out of her mouth before she could stop herself saying them as she rose very gingerly to her feet and felt every ache more acutely now the shock of landing in a morass had worn off. She recalled her sailor father muttering them under his breath when she was a girl and took a tumble when they were out on one of their long rambles through the Devon countryside, during what turned out to be her parents' last-ever shore leave before his ship was lost. Even the memory of her mother's fury with them both when Fliss innocently repeated his curses was a poignant reminder that her parents were so long dead now she sometimes found it difficult to recall what they looked like.

She was *not* going to cry, though. Luna was still loose and they had a long walk to endure in this sorry state when she found her. Tears would not help to make any of it seem less of a challenge.

'You will just have to brazen it out, Felicity,' she told herself crossly. Excited yips from the other side of the great tree spurred her into prising herself out of the mud completely and stumbling on past the soreness and bruises to the urgent business of finding her friend's dog. If only she could catch the horrid little animal, they could hurry back to Miss Donne's house and get clean again. If she was very lucky indeed, nobody would see her looking so awful and smelling this foul.

Darius Yelverton had heard those distant yelps as well, but he was furious with whoever had let a dog stray on his land. From the noise and restless movements he could hear up ahead his best ewes and lambs felt under threat from it as well. Dashing up the lane in his still-unfamiliar workingman's boots, he wished he had his army boots as well as his rifle so he could shoot the cur if it was playing the wolf with his stock.

He hated killing anything after years of doing it for his country as an officer in Wellington's Peninsular Army, but he was determined to protect his flocks and this precarious new way of life with his last breath. He had come back home after the ill-starred Battle of Toulouse a war-weary former infantry officer without much idea of what he was going to do with the rest of his life but, please God, let it not be fighting. Then Owlet Manor and its rundown farms had fallen into his lap like a miracle and he would fight even harder than he had had to in the army to keep it.

He felt his heartbeat race with dread of what he might see and broke into a run, cursing the lie of the land, all this overgrown scrub and the high-banked stone walls blocking his view of his precious livestock. He reached the gate and heaved a sigh of relief; the sheep were milling about, calling in alarm as they clustered by the gate to get as far away from the noise of a predator nearby, but they were safe, for now. He had to catch that dratted dog before it got among them and caused terrible damage. The sight of their shepherd would have soothed the flock, but he was busy helping mend walls and fences so they could be moved closer to the house. Not being as quick at the job yet, Darius had volunteered to check on the flock for him, but as he was still more or less a stranger to them they did not quiet when he appeared. He really had to get hold of that yapping dog before it did them any more harm. It was a good thing they were not heavy with lamb at this time of year so at least they could not abort in their terror.

While he might not know every inch of his land yet, nothing had prepared him for the fierce burn of possession he felt for this rundown but almost magical place the moment he had laid eyes on it. He was never going to let the tired old manor house and rundown farms go unless someone physically wrested them from him. If he could only afford to have both of his sisters living safe under his roof at long last, he would be a very happy man.

Darius scrambled over the rickety stile and into the unkempt woods and wished he could afford a woodsman, especially when a bramble snagged his ankles and he had to stop and unwind himself from its sneaky barbs before he could hurry onwards. The noise of the confounded dog sounding almost hysterical with excitement now spurred him into a run as soon as he was free again. If the animal was after a fox it could get itself killed and maybe that would be good riddance to it—except he had seen too much death and wanton destruction in the Peninsula to shrug and pass by.

Now he could hear the scrabble of claws as the still-unseen dog shifted to get closer to whatever was provoking it. Frustratingly the path snaked round a twisted old oak tree and he slowed down as his boots squelched into a dip he was surprised was still dank with muddy water even in midsummer. Human footprints and a watery impression of human hands not quite filled in by the sluggish mud said someone else had passed this way very recently. He felt a little bit guilty that someone had fallen into a near swamp on his land, even if they had to be the neglectful owner of the yapping dog he had been cursing since he first heard it in the distance. He really must get the undergrowth cleared and the ditches re-cut before winter, even if he had to do it himself.

'Come here, you double-damned limb of Satan,' an otherwise refined female voice muttered on the other side of the tree and past another thicket of brambles. The sound of more unladylike curses made him smile as he carefully avoided following in her muddy footprints and skirted the tree root that had probably caused her to fall into the mud in the first place. 'I will string you up and carve out your liver with a spoon when I finally catch you, you triple-confounded spawn of hell,' she told the excited dog in a sweetly coaxing voice as the noise of its scrabbling paws told him it had evaded her yet again.

He rounded the bole of the vast old tree, then the brambles beyond, and got his first sight of the female supposedly in charge of the dog. She tried to outwit the sharp little terrier again and fell on her hands and knees as the dog sped past her and one of the brambles he had just cursed himself snagged her already ruined gown. He was fiercely glad she was too preoccupied to look up and see him staring at her like a dumbstruck idiot. He knew he should avert his eyes, but he *was* a man as well as a former officer and supposed gentleman. Her buxom figure and wildly tumbling red curls would have forced a furtive second glance from any sentient adult male, even before her gown was sodden with mud and dirt and clinging to her magnificent figure like a lover. Now her lush breasts and hips were clearly outlined by a filthy and wet summer gown and she had no idea he was gawping at her, but he still let his gaze linger on a Venus revealed as if she was stark naked. In the middle of his own overgrown wood as well! He could still hardly believe his eyes. Even her back view was delightful. He fought to control his inevitable masculine reaction to so much feminine temptation innocently on display.

She scrambled to her feet and darted after the small brown and white dog and the sight of her generous breasts moving under her mud-stained and lovingly clinging draperies had a fire blazing his gut. He was so fascinated by the sight of her—so blissfully unaware his darker male impulses were being stoked up by her far-too-revealed curves—that for a few moments he forgot he was a gentleman and gawped wolfishly while she darted about the clearing like a very dirty wood nymph concentrating all her efforts on the dog. He was far too fascinated by the way her lithe and slender legs contrasted with the full curves of her breast and those lushly feminine hips to take much note of the animal she was chasing. He had never seen a finer female figure in a so-called classical painting or naked in his bed and he urgently wanted this one in there right now. Except her accent had sounded refined and ladylike, despite her vocabulary, and she must have looked like a modest young lady when she set out on a country walk. That was before it went so badly wrong, as she had clearly been chasing the busy little terrier now darting away from her for hours.

And he was behaving like a satyr. He should be ashamed of himself. Even if she was a relatively innocent country wife and not the single lady he fervently hoped she was, he owed her more respect than this. He would rather not lust after another man's wife and he could not afford to keep one of his own on his current income and so many responsibilities to worry about already. Disgusted with himself for even thinking that if she was a country wife she might be fair game, he remembered the terrible violence against women he had seen the aftermath of in Spain. For a moment he hated his own sex—himself included—for lusting after a woman who had no idea he was watching her with all sorts of wrongheaded masculine needs and desires torturing his unruly body.

Serve you right to burn, he told himself sternly as he turned his eyes from the tempting spectacle of a female so intent on the nimble little beast she was chasing she had no idea he was standing here watching her with such greedy eyes.

Which is just as well, Captain Yelverton told Darius sternly. *You won't be fit to be seen until you put those ridiculous fantasies to bed. And that was not the right place to try to bury them, now was it?*

Darius argued with himself. By thinking hard of somewhere very cold and unpleasant and adding in how furious he would be if any rogue stared at either of his sisters so lustily, he overcame the worst of his animal impulses and decided to intervene before she woke up his inner devils again. Best take dog and woman by surprise, he decided, and calculated distances and obstacles like an artilleryman. Satisfied it was his best chance of success he made a dive for the dog next time it was taking evasive action and luckily he was right and he got close enough for him to catch it.

'Got you, you little demon,' he told the muscular little terrier now squirming in his arms in its desperation to get away from a complete stranger. He braced himself to be bitten and held the animal out by the scruff to keep its teeth as far away from his skin as possible until it calmed down. He had to respect whoever had taught it not to bite when seized by unknown humans and risked holding it closer so it would feel more secure as a reward. It settled into the crook of his elbow as if it was tired after a demanding morning and did a fine imitation of a docile lapdog.

'Who the deuce are you?' the muddy young woman demanded with no sign of gratitude. If she knew how much she had to be grateful for, she might be more wary about waking his inner devil while she glared at him as if she was wearing layers of respectable finery and he was intruding on her solitude.

'Does this wolf in lapdog clothing have a collar and lead, or did you rely on…' he hesitated for a moment and held the animal at arm's length again. The dog squirmed around to lick his cheek as he tucked it back into the crook of his arm and a fine watchdog she was '…*her* ladylike instincts to keep her in check? If so, they seem to have failed you both rather badly.'

'She didn't bite you, though, did she?'

'Well, no, but I dare say she would have liked to.'

'Out of shock, not nastiness,' she defended the little creature she had been cursing only seconds ago.

'And unless you keep her under control she will be shot by an irate farmer. She upset my livestock with her wild barking, so you should either learn how to keep her under control in future or stay at home.'

'I know she should be on a lead,' she said, not very apologetically. He could practically hear her fighting with an urge to argue, then snatch her dog back and flounce away. For her to even know the language he had heard before she knew he was listening she could not be anywhere near as proper as she was now trying to pretend. There had even been a few choice phrases in French and something that sounded like very low Dutch to him, so perhaps the rebel under her skin was as fiery as her hair. That idea was too arousing for his own rebel body so he forced it to the back of his mind and tried to look coolly sceptical while he waited for a better explanation.

'She is not mine,' she admitted, looking a bit shamefaced now the shock of his words had finally hit home. 'And of course she was wearing her collar and lead when we set out for a walk in the country. Maybe I did not fasten the collar tightly enough since she found it too easy to slip out of it when I was not paying her enough attention. Then she was off and away before I could grab her and I have no idea how many miles we are now from where we began. First she got on one scent, then another and here we are,' she explained as if the full force of her situation had only just hit home. 'Where is that, by the way?' she asked almost casually, eyeing him warily as if she had just realised he was a man and they were alone together in the middle of nowhere. His legs were longer than hers and unfettered by sodden skirts so he would have a lot of unfair advantages in a chase, if he was that sort of ruthless, opportunistic predator. Lucky for her he was not, but she did not know that. No wonder she was looking at him so warily now it had finally occurred to her he was a healthy male with all the needs and urges of his kind in full working order.

'Brock Wood,' he told her shortly, after an unwary glance at her, then a hasty glare at the nearest bramble thicket. She had no idea her delicious feminine figure was lovingly outlined by dirty water and Herefordshire mud. Even where the finely woven stuff was drying out it threatened to plaster earth-heavy cloth against her body and mould it lovingly as a sculptor. 'On the edge of Owlet Manor's Home Farm,' he added a bit more informatively.

'I have not the least idea where that is,' she said with a trace of despair in her voice that made him pity her situation instead of worrying about his own reaction to her delightfully outlined body. Somehow he had to persuade her she could trust him far enough to come back to the house with him so she could be fussed over and cleaned up by his sister Marianne before they took her home. Meanwhile he could fetch one of the farm horses in from the fields and have it harnessed to the gig, then he supposed he would have to drive her and her borrowed dog back to wherever she came from and try to pretend he was made of stone all the way there.

He was not quite sure he had enough stone in him when he risked a glance at her again and she was still deliciously curved and utterly feminine, despite her unusual garnish of smelly mud and pond slime. Marianne could drive better than he could and she would get this goddess in sheep's clothing home before she had been away too long for anyone to send out a search party. Whoever she was and however innocent she was of blame for her current state, he still refused to marry a passing stranger to save her reputation. He had to marry money so that his sisters would have a better future than the ones they could expect if things went on as they were.

Chapter Two

Fliss wished this tall stranger would set her on the right path, then leave her to make her way back to Miss Donne's house before the lady raised the whole town to look for her missing guest. She felt an itchy sort of shame that such a compellingly handsome and vital man had seen her in such an appalling state. Yet at the same time the cold weight of her wet skirts and sodden underpinnings made her long to be close to his warmth even on this hot summer day, simply for the sake of being warm again of course, except...

Best not even think about being close to him if you were clean, Felicity. He is a complete stranger to you after all, she told herself sternly.

And such a powerful-looking one as well as he stood there in his shirtsleeves and a pair of breeches that had seen better days. *His* boots owed nothing to Bond Street, or wherever rich and idle gentlemen got their fine and immaculately polished top boots and Hessians. He wore his work boots with an air, though, and he must have been working hard since he had set out for a day of ungentlemanly toil. Yet did Miss Felicity Grantham's secret inner self find the sight and scent of such a strong and healthy man all ruffled and lightly sweating in the middle of his day's work offensive? No, she did not. He looked more of a man than any of the fine gentlemen she had met under her last employer's roof, up to and including Lady Stratford's son and her own would-be fiancé, Viscount Stratford.

How wrong of you to think so, Felicity, her inner governess whispered disapprovingly.

She should seize His Lordship's splendid proposal with both hands and stop fantasising about passing males like this one. Although he did look to be in the prime of life, just as His Lordship was, she reminded herself hastily. Wondering about the wisdom of making a marriage of convenience with a viscount should be enough of a dilemma to stop her thinking about a work-worn stranger. It might if she could only call an image of Lord Stratford to mind. Unfortunately, she had never seen the cool and detached Lord Stratford in his shirt sleeves with mud on his boots and the smell of cattle or sheep about his person. And if His Lordship had an impressively muscled torso and arms like a timber-feller his tailor had done a good job of disguising them under exquisitely cut coats, sober waistcoats and gentlemanly pantaloons. Then there were his immaculate top boots—the ones she imagined this man wearing instead and found much too flattering on his long and muscular legs for comfort.

Stop it this instant, Felicity; Lord Stratford is dark and elegant and self-assured and should not be thought of in the same sentence as a work-mussed son of the soil like this one.

His Lordship did not have a thick pelt of tawny hair that still managed to curl wildly despite a severe military-style haircut though, or piercing ice-blue eyes that even made this man's frown seem intriguing. And was the Viscount's hair curling or straight; were his eyes brown or blue? She could not remember even when she tried to force a picture of the man into focus again so she could get this one into perspective. The vivid reality of him overpainted her inner image of a polite and dignified lord, even if she had almost agreed to marry His Lordship simply because he wanted her to. Lord Stratford was not in love with her and she had managed to fob him off with a maybe while he went to Paris to help establish the British Embassy there.

The Viscount probably had a list of attributes his Viscountess should possess to have made him offer for a former governess before he went and she suspected *well-enough looking, but not a beauty* was near the top of it, just after *sensible* and *practical* and *not too demanding*.

'Who are you?' she demanded rather rudely, but if the man was planning to ravish her he would have shown some signs of rabid male lust by now and that was hardly likely when she smelt like a swamp and felt miserably self-conscious.

'Darius Yelverton, very much at your service, madam,' he said solemnly and bowed as if she was an immaculately attired lady he had met in a drawing room.

She was right then; he must have been born a gentleman. Yet gentlemen did not work. Having demanded his name so rudely, it was only fair for her to give him hers in return, though, gentleman or no. 'I am Miss Grantham and I am staying in Broadley Town with a good friend of mine. The fine little actress in your arms is my friend Miss Donne's pet dog and she is very welcome to her since *I* want nothing more to do with you, you wretched little turncoat,' she said sternly. Luna just about managed a desultory wag of her stubby tail, then sighed blissfully as Mr Yelverton rubbed her ear in exactly the right place. 'I suppose whatever she was chasing must be miles away by now,' Fliss said to stop herself having any more wicked thoughts about how it might feel for her to be so gently caressed by him instead.

'I have no idea what she was chasing all the way out here, but I suspect one of the farm cats must have been enjoying itself at her expense just now. They are wild and scratch and bite everyone but my sister, who will insist on feeding them so well they prefer teasing the farm dogs to catching vermin nowadays.'

'I dare say you are right, then, and while I must thank you very sincerely for catching Luna for me, sir, I really must get her home now. If you would be kind enough to hold her still while I fasten her collar and lead on again I shall be grateful to you,' she said, trying to sound quietly composed as she brushed as much mud as possible off the supple leather of Luna's expensive collar with a handy dock leaf. She had been forced to clasp collar and lead around her neck and chest for the want of a pocket in her high-waisted gown, so of course it got muddy when she fell.

'Make sure you buckle it tightly this time,' he said as if she might be silly enough to make the same mistake twice.

'I am so glad you told me that,' she said irritably.

'And you can just keep still, you little madam,' Mr Yelverton told Luna sternly as she ducked and squirmed so Fliss had to spend far longer this close to his warm and lightly sweating male body than felt proper.

She did *not* want to feel the warmth of his skin under that robust cotton work shirt as she buckled the collar, or be haunted by the salty scent of the work he had already done today. She backed hastily away once the collar was finally fastened tightly enough to hold the little devil if she did struggle out of his arms, which looked unlikely just at the moment. At least she could now hand him the other end of the lead and step away, but she knew he had begun the day fastidiously clean and that was another item on the list of reasons her inner idiot found him far too appealing. There was no sour trace of yesterday's labour on his skin or, horrid thought, yet older days of it on him or his clothes. Someone must see he had a clean shirt to put on every day and thank goodness he was particular enough to wear it. Hopefully he had a wife as well as a sister at home and that should stop him being such a temptation to wandering ladies. Temptation! What a ridiculous word for her to define him with. She was not at all tempted by tall and muscular gentlemen with mocking silver-blue eyes that looked as if they would read her wicked thoughts like a child's primer if she did not stop having them immediately. Maybe it was a blessing her face was slicked with drying mud then, as long as it was thick enough to hide the blush she could feel scorching her redhead's giveaway pale skin.

'You can hand her over or set her on the ground now, Mr Yelverton. We two wanderers must be on our way and if you will be kind enough to tell me how to get back to Broadley I shall be even more grateful to you than I am already,' she said stiffly.

'If I can persuade you to trust I am not a foul attacker or would-be seducer I believe it would be much better if you came home with me, Miss Grantham. My sister Marianne will do her best to make you a clean and respectable young lady again so we can drive you home in our gig and nobody will think anything of it. Your friend will suffer less anxiety if you both return home neat and clean and I can send a boy with a message to say you are on your way and not to worry. I may only be a farmer now, but I hope I am still enough of a gentleman to help a lady in distress.'

The idea of being clean again and back in Broadley before she could get there on foot tugged one way, while common sense and native caution argued it was better to suffer the humiliation of being seen like this in public than take a risk on his good intentions, despite his direct steel-blue gaze and very gentlemanly dignity as he stood there defying her to find him less than he should be because he worked his own land. 'How can I be sure you even have a sister?' she asked him anyway.

'I defy anyone to invent a force of nature like Marianne, but I am actually blessed with two of them. Only Marianne lives with me, but they certainly exist,' he said with a preoccupied frown, as if his absent sister was far more of a concern than a stray young woman holding up his hard day's work. 'The older of my two sisters is called Mrs Marianne Turner and she is the widow of an old army colleague and friend. She has agreed to keep house for me, since she dearly loves a challenge and my house is certainly one of those. I must warn you Owlet Manor has been shockingly neglected. My great-uncle lived there alone after his parents died and seems to have had little regard for his own comfort. Even after six weeks of my sister clearing and scrubbing and dusting the poor old place morning, noon and night it is still very much a work in progress.'

'I am sorry for your sister's loss,' she said stiffly

and considered how horrifying it must be to lose a beloved husband to an enemy bullet or bayonet thrust. So that was why this man could stand so militarily present and correct at times—if he was with the Duke of Wellington's Peninsular force until recently she could see why he had learnt to hide his true feelings from interested strangers.

'Kind of you,' he said abruptly.

'Are you sure your sister will want a muddy and wild-looking stranger descending on her when she has so much to do?' she asked doubtfully. She was hazy about the details of life as a farmer's wife, sister or housekeeper, but dairying, cooking and maybe even a little light gardening and hen-keeping might well be part of it, as well as all that scrubbing and dusting. If Mrs Turner shared her brother's barely suppressed energy and impatience to get through all the work left undone for so many years the lady might be annoyed by such an interruption to her busy day.

'Marianne will always have a welcome ready for anyone in genuine need of her help,' he said with a wry smile that spoke of great affection for his widowed sister.

Fliss was reluctant to ask for it, though, and he was a stranger and she was used to being independent, and they *were* in the middle of nowhere. She realised the sheep nearby had calmed down so she could only hear an occasional maternal baa and an answering shriller one from a half-grown lamb. Even the birds sounded sleepy and the distant drum of a woodpecker and the occasional bark of a farm dog drifted towards them on a sudden stir of breeze. She eyed him cautiously and he looked back at her blandly, as if he wondered what else he could say to reassure her and whether he should even bother to try. 'Very well, then. Thank you for offering such hospitality to a chance met and very muddy stranger,' she said ruefully and gestured him to go first. 'You know the way,' she explained and left him with Luna to carry so that the wriggling little madam would keep his hands full if she had misread his essential character and he made a grab at her along the way. The little dog was so happy in the crook of his arm she had gone to sleep and was clearly no use whatsoever as a protector, whatever Miss Donne had said this morning about her pet's wonderful talent as a chaperon and guard dog. It felt a bit galling that he had charmed the little terrier so easily when she had been staying with her friend for a few weeks now and the dog only seemed to notice she was there when she wanted something from her.

Fliss sighed and resigned herself to an uncomfortable walk in the sticky heat of whatever time of day it was by now. They strolled along at what she was quite sure was a much slower pace than he would set on his own. They must make a very odd procession and she wondered what his old comrades would say if they could see him now. Officer Yelverton escorting one muddy lady and her dog back to his home to be dealt with by his sister. That blush stained her cheeks again under the mud when he strode over the tumbledown stile at the end of the woodland path and woke up those silly fantasies in her stupid, misguided head all over again. He had tucked Luna under one arm until he was over the hedge and now held out his other hand to help Fliss over the step in her dirt-sodden and surprisingly heavy skirts. He looked impassive, but Luna seemed cross about being woken up and stared reproachfully at Fliss as if it was her fault. Vexed by the dog's convenient memory, she scrambled over the stile with her skirts held in one hand while she grasped Mr Yelverton's strong and work-calloused one with the other. She had to lean more of her weight on him than she wanted to in order to avoid tearing her gown. Although it was already ruined, the thought of rambling around the countryside with a great rent in it as well as all the mud weighing it down made her quail. The feel of his firm, warm male hand under her palm was intimate and rather heady and added yet another layer to the temptation she had hardly even known existed until today. She had never felt anything close to this jag of awareness at the mere touch of a man's bare skin against hers until now. In truth, she had not been used to much masculine company at all, but something still told her this one was exceptional and clinging to his strength after so many misadventures felt far too much of a temptation.

'Thank you,' she said breathlessly as soon as she

was standing on solid ground. She pretended to look at the high stone walls as she willed her heartbeat to slow and her breathing to steady. Not that there was very much to see. 'The lanes around here are very deep, are they not?' she said more or less at random.

'This track is the dividing line between one farm and another so I suppose it must be very old to have been worn so deeply.'

'These banks and wall certainly hide most of the land from our view.'

'Probably just as well; the farms are not quite as neglected as my house, but there are too many this-tles and rushes and nettles about for me to be able to feel proud of any of it yet.'

'You must find this a very different life from sol-diering.' Even from behind she saw his shoulders stiffen at her clumsy reminder of his former life and she should not make personal comments about a man she had met only minutes ago. It did not feel like that, though, and at least listening for his reply meant she did not have to dwell on the strange idea she had known deep down that he was important to her the instant she met his eyes across an overgrown clear-ing in an overgrown wood.

'My father is a clergyman and ran the glebe farm when we were young, so at least I have some idea of what to do,' he said as if he was oversensitive about the gap between soldier and farmer.

'I did not mean it as a criticism,' she said. She was the one who insisted he walk ahead of her, so it was her own fault if she found talking to his back frustrating. 'And it must seem like a very quiet life after the hustle and bustle of the army.'

'Indeed it does and that's what I was looking for when I sold out after the Battle of Toulouse, determined never to fight in another battle. I should not complain about the state of this windfall that has fallen into my lap so unexpectedly, thanks to my late great-uncle's generosity in naming me his heir.'

'You must feel torn between missing him and wanting to get this place in good order as fast as can be,' she said more warily.

'As I had never set eyes on the gentleman I can hardly miss him, although living in his house does sometimes feel as if I inhabit his shell. It sounds a fanciful idea, but his presence is sometimes so strong at Owlet Manor that I almost expect to turn round and see him glaring at me for all the upheaval and our new-fangled ideas about his house and farms. My mother claims her uncle was a recluse even when she was a little girl and recalls being brought here by her parents, hoping he would take to the only child of her generation as his heiress. She claims he ordered her to stop her chatter and told her parents to take her away and leave him alone and if he wanted to be deafened by a widgeon he would go and sit in the henhouse. She avoided him from that moment on and I can hardly blame her, but he did leave me a letter saying it was only because I did not toady or try to see him that he left me Owlet Manor and the land so I have a lot to thank her for because she took him at his word. It feels a little unjust I benefited so much when I only had a vague idea he existed and my sisters had left him alone as well.'

'It sounds a fine heritage,' she said, her own recent inheritance on her mind.

'It is; I am a very lucky man.'

She was silent for a while since he had left her nothing to say. He had been lucky to inherit so much, but the state of the wood and the fact he was working so hard on his own farmland argued this place was not exactly proving to be a goldmine. They strode on—him looking preoccupied with his responsibilities and his acres, her swatting away flies and hating the feel of all this dirt on her skin and even in her hair. If she could think of something else to talk about, she might not feel so self-conscious and troubled by all her aches and scrapes now she had time to think about them. It was silly to feel safe inside these strong sandstone walls with a strong man to protect her when he was only a chance-met stranger and she could look after herself, most of the time. She felt alive in every pore and far too aware of him and it was time she stopped wondering how it might feel to stroll here with him and be clean and feel feminine next to him arm in arm, instead of follow-my-leader and about as dirty as she could be while he walked in front and tried not to breathe in her stench.

'Your sheep have settled down,' she remarked more or less at random as they paused at the first gateway into the fields so he could check on his flock. 'I am very sorry that Luna's barking disturbed them so.'

'Aye, it is far too hot for them today and I came too late in the year to hire a good team of shearers to work on my flocks until they have finished everyone else's, so now I have to wait until next week before they can start,' he said, as if he was far more interested in his sheep than the disruptive female taking up so much of his time on a busy day.

'You have more than one flock, then?' she asked, trying to take a polite interest in his farms since he was kind enough to take time to help her.

'Aye, these are pure Ryelands and the others are Ryeland-cross-Cotswolds, and they are all too heavy with wool for this time of year. I have no idea how my uncle thought they were going to get shorn if he did not engage a competent team of shearers in good time, or why he did not ask whoever he had last year to come back and do it again.'

'Are they held to be good examples of their breed?' she asked as the ways of reclusive elderly gentlemen were beyond her, too. 'They look as if they had spent the night at rather a wild ball with their curly fleeces and those curious topknots.'

'Aye, you're right, they do,' he said with a delighted smile as if he had been looking for the right words to describe them since he got here.

She caught herself grinning back at him like an

idiot and managed to tear her gaze away and eye the sheep up again as if they fascinated her.

'They are not excellent yet, but not terrible either,' he said in answer to her question and now he was frowning again when she chanced a sidelong glance. 'Those who know a great deal more about sheep than I do tell me I must beg, borrow or buy a new ram by the autumn if I want to improve their bloodlines, but I doubt breeding sheep is considered a proper topic of conversation for a refined lady so we had best change the subject.'

'Oh, for goodness sake, why will people pretend we women are incapable of facing the truths of life simply because some of us are lucky enough not to have to dig or spin for a living?' Fliss said impulsively. He looked uncomfortable with her attempt to tear down some of the social barriers between ladies and gentlemen and right now she supposed she ought to agree with him. Not that she could be much temptation to be over-familiar with as filthy and smelly as she was now.

'The niceties of life keep us civil and civilised,' he said dourly and seemed to be making an effort not to look at her disgracefully muddy and unkempt person.

Was he repulsed by her deplorable state or trying to deny her right to speak as a human being rather than an easily shocked lady? Or could he possibly mean she aroused uncivilised thoughts in his manly bosom? Wrinkling her nose at the smell of dank mud and sweaty and overset woman, she very much doubted it.

Chapter Three

'Shall we carry on?' he said patiently, as if he had satisfied himself his sheep were settled and he had best get this duty to help a stranger over with as fast as possible.

'The sooner the better,' she said briskly and waited for him to lead the way again. So they trudged along the closed-in lane in silence. How would it be if he wanted to be with her? she mused to divert herself from the bruises and scrapes on her knees and hands. Best not know how filthy her feet were, but she regretted not looking down at them when she stumbled on a rough area where rainwater had carved a gully.

'Are you all right?' he stopped long enough to turn and ask her.

She waved a hand to tell him it was nothing. 'I am perfectly well, thank you,' she lied airily, even if a childish part of her longed for a shady corner and the peace to have a good weep over the fiasco her day had turned into. 'Best if I pay more attention to where I am going from now on, though, and stop trying to see over the walls.'

'When we reach the next bend in the path there I can promise you a fine view across the valley and down to Owlet Manor and there will not be much further to go once we get there,' he said encouragingly and turned to lead the way again.

'Is your house very picturesque?' she asked the back of his head. If he had insisted on her going first he would have to look at her back view instead and what a filthy and unkempt sight that would be for him whenever he looked up. And she was surrounded by a whole cloud of flies attracted by the stench of stagnant mud and overheated human, so he must be doubly glad he was ahead and not behind her.

'To me it is nigh perfect,' he said ruefully as they entered a stretch of the track blissfully shadowed by the dappled shade cast by rowan and birch trees, 'and, yes, very picturesque, although not that comfortable or convenient at the moment and a century or two out of date.'

'It sounds lovely,' she said politely, keeping up the pretence they were taking a quiet stroll on a warm day and making idle conversation about his new home.

'It is old fashioned and neglected, but I doubt I will be bored for at least a couple of decades and, as I said before, I never even dreamt I might inherit such a fine old place one day, so I am not an impartial witness.'

'You must have stayed in some odd places when you were with the army on campaign,' she said to keep this polite thread going while she trudged up a gentle enough slope. She hoped they were near his promised viewing point and she could have a rest at last as she felt very weary now. His legs were longer than hers and she did not want to have to gasp out a plea for him to slow down when she wanted to get to his home and be clean again rather urgently as well.

'Aye,' he said somberly, as if looking back on the hard and unpredictable life it must have been and expecting to wake up one day and find this was only a dream.

She slapped at a persistent fly and sighed. Never had being clean and well groomed seemed such a luxury. Then he stopped at the crown of the hill and she was glad to get her breath back before she could spare attention for the generous view.

'There,' he said, a touch of apprehension in his silver-blue eyes, as if it mattered to him what she thought of his home and that was downright fanciful of her. 'Owlet Manor is over there, at the foot of the southern slope.'

'It is such a beautiful valley and the house looks so perfect from up here,' she said with genuine awe. A substantial brick, timber and plaster manor house was cradled among trees and meadows and what looked like an extensive orchard down there in the valley bottom. It was obviously very old and surrounded by mellow redbrick and stone barns and stables of a very similar age. There was even a tiny church beyond it to add to its air of self-sufficient contentment as it basked in the summer sun, as if warming its old bones. Even from up here she could see how the oak timbers had weathered to a silvery grey and, looking more closely, she noted that almost half of the panels of plaster shone brighter and must have been whitewashed recently. Of course Mr Yelverton and his sister would be in a hurry to protect his splendid old house from the elements before autumn gales swooped down the valley to buffet it. Valuing that venerable old house only added to his appeal to her mind and senses, though, and he was far too attractive for them already. 'Is that a moat?' she asked as a sparkle of sun on water shimmered around the main house in a snatch of breeze.

'Not now, although it might well have been once upon a time. I suppose when the Marches were thick with pikes, swords and rival armies it would have felt safer to have a stretch of water between you and the local robber barons. There is only a small lake at one side of the house now and I keep thinking my sister will unearth some old maps or plans to show us how it was, but she has not done so as yet. My great-uncle seems as likely to have kept important family papers in an attic or cellar or a horse stall as to have put them anywhere you might expect to find them.'

'He sounds like rather an eccentric gentleman.'

'He was not the only one,' he said gloomily. 'The entire Peacey family seem to have hoarded every piece of cracked china or worn-out furniture that crossed their threshold since the house was built. Great-Uncle Hubert has only added the top layers of the ancient lumber my sister is working her way through room by room. I suppose it is as well she is here to stop me adding to it and leaving the rest to addle, until I pass away a bad-tempered recluse in my ninetieth year and someone else has to tidy up after another reclusive squire of Owlet Manor.'

'Do you feel there is a danger of you doing that?' Fliss asked before she could remind herself not to ask personal questions. He would certainly not stay unwed long if the local beauties set eyes on him, crumbling old house and neglected farms or not.

'There is so much to do that I could forget the rest of the world if I was not careful,' he said absently, as if brooding over which task was next on his list trumped taking offence, or even listening very hard to what she had to say.

Apparently it trumped meeting his neighbours as well, since she would have noticed him at any of the local celebrations of the peace Miss Donne had insisted on attending, so Fliss would not be bored. Although Fliss secretly suspected Miss Donne was happy to have an excuse to gad about the neighbourhood and enjoy those parties herself, now she had retired and did not need to set a good example to the young ladies in her charge any longer.

'I know I am no expert, but the hedges and field

walls here look quite well maintained to me,' she said doggedly taking an interest in them instead of him.

'It is unusual to enclose common land here, so fortunately there are not all that many to maintain. If we landowners were to fence in the woods and wastes, the local people would be certain to starve on the pittance we can afford to pay them in this remote part of the country,' he said and she was glad he was not a grasping landowner happy to enrich himself at the cost of poor commoners.

'It does seem wrong to take away what little extra a man can make spin out after a long day's work, then expect him to feed his family on even less when life is so hard for them already even in more prosperous places closer to the big cities.'

'It is iniquitous,' he said abruptly.

She felt guilty about living in great houses on prosperous estates for most of her life, even if she had never quite been part of those noble households as first a dependent and unwanted orphan, then as a governess. She was almost glad when he turned his back on the view and frowned briefly before giving her an almost polite nod and leading the way downhill again. He seemed intent on getting home as fast as possible so he could be rid of her now. Trying to ignore her bruises, sore feet and the hot sun on her back, she trudged in his wake, dreaming of cool, clear water and soap, maybe even rosewater, or lavender oil to take away the stench of eau de mud from her skin and hair. And clean clothes so fine they would drift and drape around her with every breath of a breeze and fascinate any stray gentlemen awe-struck by her transformation from frog woman into fairy princess. Well, she could dream.

'Good heavens above, Darius, whatever have you been up to this time?' demanded the tall girl whom Fliss had taken for a housemaid at first glance, as she took in the strange little procession that emerged from the overgrown orchard and into the drying yard behind the house.

Since no maid would dare address her employer so abruptly this must be his sister, even if she was dressed in an old-fashioned cotton gown, rough apron and a cobweb-and-dust-strewn mobcap. She had been beating what looked like a very old carpet when they walked through the gate, but dropped the stout stick she was using to beat it with and came to have a closer look at the female scarecrow her brother had brought home with him.

'Nothing to do with me, Marianne; Miss Grantham had got herself in this state before we even met, so you cannot lay her ills at my door.'

'And if only you were wearing a jacket I am sure you would have given it to Miss Grantham to wear and hide some of the damage,' his sister said as if it had to be his fault in some way and she surprised Fliss into hiding a smile she had not thought she had anywhere about her person until she was clean again and had something to smile about.

'As I was not wearing one I could hardly hand it over to her, could I? And there was nobody to see her except me anyway.' The other woman rolled her eyes at Fliss to say she had heard the wrong in that statement and sympathised with Fliss for having to walk however far they had come with such an idiot for company. 'But never mind berating me for my sins of omission,' he went on regardless. 'Is there any hot water left in the copper for Miss Grantham to bathe in?'

The lady nodded and Fliss could not bite back a sigh of relief. The very thought of being able to wash some of this horrible mud off her person and out of her hair sounded like heaven to her and she was tempted to walk into the stretch of water she could see through the stand of trees at the end of the orchard and be rid of some of it right now. She might come out with nearly as much mud and some extra pond weed so she just managed to stop herself running past them both and throwing herself in.

'Good. I had best keep this demon dog in check while you find Miss Grantham a place to bathe in peace and quiet, Nan. Then once I have carried the buckets in I will fetch one of the horses in so we can drive them both back to Broadley as soon as may be,' he added gruffly.

'One thing at a time, Captain Yelverton,' his sister replied and at least now Fliss knew what his rank had been. Marianne sounded well used to overriding her bossy and impatient brother's orders. 'First, you must haul the hip bath into the little parlour so we can close the shutters against the sun and any impudent rogues who might intrude on a lady's privacy. Then, after you have filled it with the copper of hot water I got ready to use to scrub the floor in the front parlour now it has been cleared for the first time in about a century, you can draw more water from the well to heat up again so I may bathe and be clean enough to drive into town as your chaperon. We will need to dunk this grubby little animal in my bath water so she is a more acceptable companion on the journey than she would be right now as well. Life is rarely as straightforward as you men think it ought to be, Brother dear,' she said as he sighed at her list of tasks to be done before he could be comfortable again.

'As I am going to be so busy, let us hope you will not make too much fuss about being shut in the stables while all that happens then, young lady,' he said to the dog, as if he was more comfortable talking to her than his sister and an inconvenient stranger like Fliss.

'I don't care if she minds or not, she got me into this mess in the first place,' Fliss said crossly.

'True, but I have no time to dash around the countryside looking for her if we are to get you both home before midnight,' he said and Fliss could practically hear him adding *And look what happened when you did it* under his breath.

'I could feed her some scraps to make her more

contented while you are busy,' his sister told him
with a severe look to say he was being rude to their
surprise visitor. 'I expect you would like something
to eat after such a tiring day, wouldn't you, darling?'
the lady said to the little dog and Fliss had not even
known she was hungry until now. She began to wonder if naughty dogs were more important here than
muddy young women who had drying mud smeared
in places she did not even want to think about right
now.

'Please refrain from making the little wretch so
comfortable she keeps trying to come here on her
own and causes even more mayhem than she has
today,' Mr Yelverton warned his sister, then walked
off to the farmhouse with Luna tucked under his
arm and not even a glance behind him to see if they
were following.

'Do you think he means me or the dog?' Fliss
muttered with an infuriated glare at his broad back.

'Oh, definitely the dog, he knows we cannot keep
you.'

There was a moment of awkward silence while
Fliss wondered whether to be offended and decided
it was too much trouble and laughed instead. She
liked Mr Yelverton's forthright sister. 'At least there
is one thing to be thankful for today, then,' she said
with a rueful shrug.

'Do forgive me; I often say things I should keep
to myself. My mother despairs of me, but at least she
cannot even try to turn me into a proper lady now

I am here and she is miles away in Bath. So please don't take offence and forgive us for being such poor hosts. Darius is embarrassed by the state of his house and I expect that is why he is being even more of a gruff bear than he usually is,' Marianne said with a wry grimace that said a lot about her opinion of his delicate manly sensibilities. 'And he forgot to introduce us properly. I am Marianne Turner, Miss Grantham...' She paused and shrugged as if facing a duty she did not relish, but refused to sidestep. 'I might as well warn you that I put myself beyond the pale seven years ago by running off with my brother's sergeant and marrying him at the drumhead despite his scruples and my parents' dire warnings of disaster. I have never regretted a single moment of my life with my husband, only that Daniel is dead and buried in a far-off land and I miss him like the devil. I refuse to bury my sins in his grave and pretend it never happened, especially as they never felt like sins while he was alive, or at any time since for that matter. My mother and father are so ashamed of my marriage they would rather deny it ever happened, but I refused to lie our love out of existence so it was a huge relief to us all when Darius invited me to help him fight the dust of ages and make this lovely old house into a home again. And I talk too much as well.'

Feeling as if she was being expected to face one more difficult obstacle between her and that bath she longed for when she was dazed with weariness and horribly dirty, Fliss searched for the right words. Marianne Turner looked as if she regretted telling her the truth, even if she would never regret the life she had with her late husband. 'I cannot imagine why your mother and father were so against the marriage when he obviously made you happy. It is not as if you ran away without marrying him and I admire you for following your heart. You did what you needed to do in order to marry your sweetheart and just think how bitterly you would regret it now if you had stayed at home and done as you were told.'

Marianne gave a great sigh, as if she had been dreading saying her piece to the first lady who crossed her path ever since she came here. 'I knew I was going to like you,' she said. 'Anyone who could get as dirty as you are and not cry or have an attack of the vapours about it cannot be anything like the ladies who used to look down their noses at me in Bath.'

'And you have dust all over your mobcap and a streak of it down the side of your face, so it's not as if you have much room to talk about my dirt,' Fliss said and supposed the lack of tear tracks among the mud and grime on her own cheeks was something to be thankful for after all. Just as well her urgent need to find Luna, then Mr Yelverton's manly presence, saved her from one humiliation then.

Chapter Four

Darius could hear the murmur of feminine voices outside in the garden as his sister chatted to Miss Grantham as if they were already friends and he did as he was bid. He heaved the hip bath into the small parlour, then filled the tub with hot water as fast as he could get it there without spilling too much of it. Marianne would have to find soap and wash cloths and any bits of this and that a lady like Miss Grantham would need to feel properly clean again.

He tried hard to think about the farms and all the urgent tasks awaiting him, but his inner rake kept wondering how she would look stripped of her ruined gown and everything she had on underneath it. He had to keep reminding himself she was a lady and strictly off limits for a rough farmer like him. It was not her fault she aroused his basest masculine urges the first moment he saw her across that clearing. Those urges were tugging at his resolution to be a proper gentleman every time he thought about her naked even now.

She clearly had no idea how lushly appealing her curvaceous figure was to the likes of him, but at least a cleaner and less-revealed lady would stand in her ruined shoes when she had to put them on again. He could not imagine Marianne's shoes fitting a lady six inches shorter then she was and that had him thinking about Miss Grantham, the pocket Venus, all over again. That was not at all what he wanted when he had to be fit for mixed company as soon as they had finished their chat and come in to find out how he was doing with Marianne's latest list of works.

Then Miss Grantham came to the back door to warily watch Marianne feed the little dog. Luna ate ravenously, drank thirstily and looked around for a place to sleep off her busy morning and Darius was glad of the excuse of making sure the cold water in the large jug he was carrying did not spill on to the scrubbed brick floor so he could avoid looking at Miss Grantham and his sex becoming fully aroused again. 'Your bath will soon be ready for you, my lady,' he said as lightly as he could manage under the circumstances.

'Thank you, kind sir,' she said and she was a gallant female, wasn't she?

'My pleasure, ma'am.'

'I doubt it, Mr Yelverton, but thank you for pretending. I know what a nuisance Luna and I are being to you and your sister.'

'Nonsense.' Marianne dismissed all his trouble and this uneasy wanting he was fighting with an impatient snap of her fingers as she stepped past her new friend and took a critical look around her kitchen as if he might not even be capable of filling a lady's bath without sisterly supervision. 'We are glad of the company and both of us need to practise our social skills before we turn into a pair of grumpy old recluses like our great-uncle.'

'Speak for yourself,' Darius muttered as he ferried another jug of ice-cold well water into Miss Grantham's makeshift bathing chamber and tried to halt his wayward imagination. Outside and sharing a light-hearted conversation with his sister she had only been a prickle of awareness under his skin, but even in the shade inside the house he could almost see through the mud and cloth to the woman underneath as she stood hesitating by the door with the sun behind her. He would soon be embarrassingly rampant again if she did not come inside. At least Marianne was too busy unearthing washing balls and towels to cast him a knowing look. And Miss Grantham had no idea what a temptation she was to a battered former soldier who had obviously not managed to beg or charm his way into a woman's bed for far too long.

'You had best come inside, Miss Grantham,' he told her gruffly. 'Marianne will soon find you everything you will need and bring it in to you, then guard the door against all comers. After her experiences in the Peninsula she understands exactly how you are feeling right now and one thing I do know is that you will never get clean if you skulk in the yard for the rest of the day. We can hardly throw buckets of water over you until you think you might be clean enough to risk tiptoeing across my sister's nice clean floor.'

'It will hardly be so after I have tracked mud and dust all over it, but thank you anyway,' she said stiffly and came inside by about two steps and stopped as if she felt the tension in the air between them as acutely as he did.

Impossible, he told himself, she was a respectable female in very trying circumstances and of course she was self-conscious and tongue-tied with him now they were actually at Owlet Manor. 'You are welcome,' he said almost truthfully.

'There, I think I have thought of everything you will want for now,' Marianne said as she came back into the room and frowned at Darius as if she could not imagine why he was still here. 'I will leave you to your bath and try to find something clean for you to wear while you are busy,' she said pointedly to Miss Grantham and not him.

'I *am* supposed to refill the copper from the well, remember?' he said to her back.

'There is an outside door to the scullery though, isn't there?' Marianne said flatly and she was quite right, there was. He was the one who had had to take it off its hinges and plane it into the right misshape to fit the equally twisted doorjamb when they got here and she had insisted on it functioning to save whoever had to fill the copper tracking through her kitchen.

'And you would have given me the rough side of your tongue if I forgot to take in cold water as well as hot, would you not, sister dear?'

'It is good for you to be humbled every now and again, Captain, so why not go and do as you are bid for once, Darius?'

'It's just like being in the army again,' he said disgustedly and picked up the other empty bucket and stumped through the scullery door, then shut it behind him with such restraint they ought to know he wanted to slam it so hard the windows rattled.

It was unusual to see such dark eyes combined with Miss Grantham's fiery locks, Darius mused as he marched to the well and drew water as fast as he could lift the buckets out. Of course he was trying to distract himself from a sensual inner picture of him being in there with her, in that tight little tub and a shadowy private room, with no Marianne about to guard her new friend's privacy from rogues like him. So were Miss Grantham's eyes darkest velvet brown or deep, dark blue at close quarters? There had been no question of him peering down at her to find out when they first set eyes on each other and he doubted she had looked him properly in the face all the time they were walking here or since they had arrived at the manor house. Despite that avoidance his inner fantasist imagined her shooting a languishing, inviting look his way from darkest-brown or deepest-blue eyes under steam-spiked and ridiculously long lashes, preferably over a bare and soap-slicked shoulder to make it seem even more enticing. It would be a look that beckoned him to act as her bathroom attendant and lover when he joined in her ablutions and never mind a few splashes on Marianne's immaculately scrubbed floor as they explored one another as lovers in the intimate and steamy half-light of the shuttered and intimate parlour. No, it was not even to be thought of, nor pictured so vividly it could be real, if he tried hard enough to envision every move, every sigh and sweet little moan of encouragement as they came together in the ultimate intimacy. And they would need a much cleaner bath than hers would be as soon as she had been in it long to satisfy his sinful longings, even if they were reciprocated. He very much doubted she knew what a sinful longing was. Not that his inner satyr would care if he could join her in that tub of steamy water and lure her into a dirty game of them as lovers, eagerly satisfying one another among breathy sighs and splashes and soap bubbles and never mind the state of the water.

Damn it, he was hard as rock and tempted to pour the latest bucket of ice-cold water over himself out here in the yard to cool his inner demons down. He could only have a lady like her if he married her first. The last thing he needed was a wife who would divert him from all the things he should be doing elsewhere with one inviting look over her slender shoulder. If he was ever going to save his sisters from a life of hard work and genteel poverty, he would have to work hard and wed a decent fortune as well. Miss Grantham would be a congenial friend for his elder sister, if she was broad minded enough to accept Marianne had loved her Daniel passionately, and that was all. She could never mean anything more to him. He was not going to let any woman love him, not after watching his beloved elder sister grieve for Daniel as if she was broken and dead inside for all those terrible weeks before he finally got some of his back pay and could afford to send her home. It had torn his heart every morning she faced him blank-faced and red-eyed and pretended she was perfectly well; there was nothing wrong with her that time would not cure. He doubted it; even now he doubted it to his very heart and soul. His sister had been a loving and devoted wife and Daniel had worshipped the very ground she walked on. His brother-in-law was an exceptional man, he had realised with hindsight—a warrior with a heart as soft as butter whenever he was not in battle. Who could ever replace her beloved Dan in Marianne's heart and scout the shadows from her eyes? She loved him so much it sometimes seemed to Darius she actually had walked through hell for him on the march. So, knowing what love had done to his sister, why on earth would he want it for any female he cared for when he knew how uncertain life was at first hand? Why would he risk putting a woman like Miss Grantham through what Marianne had endured for his unworthy sake? Not that she seemed that impressed by Farmer Yelverton and he did not blame her. Love was not for him, sentimental novels and poets were welcome to it and he was hardly the stuff of any girlish dreams the lady still had, so that was just as well.

'Darius has always been as grumpy as a bear whenever he feels he might be in danger of being thanked for some kindness he has carried out,' Marianne told Fliss after her brother left as if he was impatient to be done with Fliss so he could get on with more important matters, such as his sheep and fences.

'Darius,' Fliss said thoughtfully, trying to divert herself from his brusqueness when he really must be very busy with several farms to get back in profit and this old house to rescue from neglect and decay, 'what an unusual name.'

'My father admired Herodotus's description of Darius the Great as a man with great courage in battle and determined to pursue justice for all under his rule. My brother was mad for the army as a boy and hates injustice to this day.'

'He told me he had seen enough of soldiering in the late wars,' Fliss said a little bit too quickly to be truly uninterested in dashing Captain Darius or intriguing Farmer Yelverton and his sister was sure to notice her eagerness to talk about him if she wasn't more careful.

She tried not to think about the terrible dangers and appalling sights he must have suffered from and seen. Now he was out of the way the horrid notion he could so easily have been killed on one of those far-away battlefields was haunting her like a bad smell and she shuddered and felt the pull of dry mud all over her skin. She had her own bad smell to worry about, now she came to think about it; the strong aroma of stagnant mud she had brought into her new friend's otherwise immaculate kitchen would carry into the shady and shuttered room on the other side of the oak-panelled hallway as soon as she could nerve herself to spoil that pristine tiled floor and run towards that bath. Despite her shame at making her new friend's home so noxious, she could hardly wait to get as much of the mud and stench off her person as possible.

'As well he might,' Marianne said with a sad shake of her honey-blonde head. Fliss hoped she had not reminded her new friend of her own hardships and loss when she followed the drum, but of course she must have done. Such a deep and desperate grief must always be with her now she had lost the husband she had clearly adored. 'The water will be too cold to get all the dirt off if you don't hurry up and get into your bath,' Marianne said bracingly, as if that was enough of that sad subject and they had the here and now to worry about. 'As there are no men

about to see you it might be best if you stripped off
in here so you don't have to smell your filthy clothes
while you bathe. I can put them in the copper to boil
once everyone has had their baths and washes and
maybe something can be saved from the wreckage.'

'I doubt it,' Fliss said as she looked down at the
mud and green slime and knew all too well it had
soaked right through to her skin underneath. She
felt shy of stripping naked even in front of another
woman, but Marianne was right. And it took her new
friend's help and encouragement to prise her out of
her stiff-with-dirt clothes and never mind worrying
about maidenly modesty. By the time they peeled
away Fliss's stiff and filthy cambric gown, the no-
longer-fine lawn petticoat underneath it and her
ruined corset and chemise, she was so glad to be rid
of them she forgot to care she was all but naked as the
blessedly cool and fresh air from the half-shuttered
windows caressed her muddy and overheated skin.
It even seemed funny when Marianne had to steel
herself to cut through the knots of her mud-tightened
and already ruined garters and Fliss's torn and no-
longer-in-the-least-bit-white-cotton stockings could
finally come off.

'Now I will have to try to scrub myself clean,'
Fliss said with a rueful glance down her mud-
streaked and filthy legs.

Luckily Marianne's tales of her own misadventures in Portugal and Spain when she was following
her husband on the march made this feel almost run

of the mill, but Fliss still felt vulnerable and a little bit sinful when they crossed the hall to that shadowy parlour. The muted sunlight inside the house made the shadows seem inquisitive, as if the ghosts of the past were curious about this filthy and scandalously nude visitor to their ancient home. 'My uncle said I was not to be pampered with help dressing or undressing when I was growing up as I would have to earn my own living one day,' she explained to Marianne. 'So I am not used to being stark naked in company.'

'And our maids would have looked startled and asked what was wrong with our hands if we had expected them to dress or undress us, but at least I had a sister to help me if I needed it, when she was not being an annoying little brat.'

'I would have loved a sister. My cousin is only a month or two older than I am, but she was always so jealous of her position as the daughter of the house that she all but ignored me while we were growing up under the same roof.'

'Are you an orphan, then?'

'Yes, my parents died in an explosion on board ship when I was nine. An unlucky shot at the powder magazine or some mistake or dreadful accident, I suppose. I never wanted to know all the details since nothing was ever going to bring them back.'

'Best not to know,' Marianne said dourly.

Losing her parents had been terrible enough, but to find your husband's corpse after such a notoriously bloody siege must have been appalling. There were no right words to say about a loss like that. And at least worrying about Marianne's grieving heart had got Fliss inside the little parlour and that blissful bath without worrying about being in a state of nature and she was very glad of the other woman's help with scrubbing every last speck of mud off her filthy feet. Thank goodness the rest came off more easily or she might be bright red all over before the stench was finally off her wincing skin. Marianne insisted on more gentle treatment for her grazed hands and knees and even stayed to help her wash her hair. She worked the mud out of it far more patiently than Fliss would have done. Then they rinsed it and the rest of her with cold water, since the bath water was far too dirty to be any help by then. Shivering, but feeling clean again at long last, Fliss was almost her old self again as she stepped out of the now-filthy bath water. Once she had dried herself off as best she could and wrapped a towel around her soaking wet hair Marianne passed her a fine linen shift that looked ancient but spotless and she shrugged it on with a blissful sigh. Marianne must have resurrected it from a long-forgotten chest at some point over the last few weeks and she was very grateful for its clean softness, even if all the washing and hanging out in the sun could not quite get the beautifully embroidered undergarment white again.

'Were you planning on making it into something for yourself?' she asked.

'No, I simply could not bring myself to throw it away. There is so much here that was cast aside and forgotten it seems criminal not to use anything that could be useful again and at least this time I was right. I must remember to tell Darius so when he teases me about hoarding things nobody has had a use for in all the decades it has been sitting here forgotten.'

'In this instance he is quite wrong,' Fliss said. 'I am very glad you rescued this and had it laundered. I feel gloriously clean and almost decent again.'

'You are very welcome to it then, Miss Grantham.'

'Please do not call me so after you have helped me rid myself of so much mud and grime and been so kind. I hope we can consider ourselves friends now, even if we have only just met. You have seen me naked and not even my former governess has done that and she has been my friend for years. And my given name is Felicity, but my parents and now my friends call me Fliss.'

'Fliss is a pretty name, but are you sure?'

Fliss nodded, sad that her new friend must have been slighted by far too many narrow-minded ladies after her unequal marriage for her to be so diffident about an offer of friendship. 'I should not have said so otherwise,' she said.

'Very well, I will call you that as well then. I always thought the name Felicity sounded like a reproach to those of us who are not quite so felicitous.

Was your father the son of a preacher to give you such a virtuous name?'

'No, it was his mother's name. He asked my mother to have me christened with it if he was still away from home when I was born, since she did consent to be left behind when he sailed just that one time since she was expecting me. She used to tease him that she wanted to call me Titania after the Queen of the Fairies from *A Midsummer Night's Dream* as I was born on Midsummer Day, but a promise was a promise. At least I think she was joking, but I am glad he got his way in case she was serious for once.'

'She sounds like fun,' Marianne said rather wistfully.

Fliss supposed Mrs Yelverton was not and felt blessed to have such happy memories of her own mother, even if she had lost her far too young. 'She was; they both were. They had to elope together because my grandfather had a very grand marriage planned for her and Papa was an orphan as well, but we were all very happy on shore and aboard ship.'

'You went with them?'

'Yes, at first I was too young to be left behind and apparently I travelled the oceans before I was old enough to know a midden from a topsail. Papa always used to say I was born with sea legs.'

'All I recall of the sea is being tossed about on it like a cork through the Bay of Biscay. It was rough all the way to Portugal and back again and I doubt if

I would ever grow used to it if I had to stay aboard ship for years.'

'You would in the end; Lord Nelson used to suffer from seasickness until he got his sea legs again and look what a great admiral he was. I expect troop ships are lubberly sort of craft and not a bit like the fine frigates we used to sail on. They would seem to dance over the water as much as sail it when there was a fair wind. Flying before the wind was something I missed so badly when I had to be quiet and good in my uncle's house after my parents decided I was too old to go to sea and needed an education. They were killed soon after that and I sometimes used to wish they had taken me with them when my uncle made it clear what a burden I was to him and life seemed so grim, until Miss Donne made me realise I was not alone after all. I suppose she has been my family ever since.'

'And I am very glad you are still here, even if I cannot quite understand how anyone could love being at sea,' Marianne said with a shake of the head.

'Never mind my odd ways now, do you have anything else I could borrow for our trip to Broadley?' Fliss asked wryly, waving a hand at her barely covered body.

'Nothing of mine would fit you. I suppose we could cut the skirts of one of my gowns down and try to stretch out the bodice with the bottom six inches we had to cut off,' Marianne said, gesturing at her own tall and rather willowy figure. She shot Fliss a measuring glance and shook her head. 'We could not make it work without a lot more time to fit it to your figure,' she added regretfully.

'No,' Fliss said, comparing Marianne's elegant figure with her own and wishing she was tall and gracefully curved rather than full-figured and dumpy.

'My sister Viola is much more petite than me and she left two of her best muslins with me for safekeeping, since she thinks them much too fine for a governess to wear even on high days and holidays. If she had left them in Bath with our mother, she would be sure to cut them up to make christening gowns for the poor. Mama cannot put aside thirty years as a vicar's wife even now my father has had to retire for the sake of his health and never mind what Viola would wear at the Upper Rooms when she came home. I have the gowns stored in the bedchamber I have finally managed to get clean and ready for her to use if she can ever manage to come and stay. She would be the first to insist you wear one of them rather than go about in a flour sack or wrapped in my cloak to hide your nakedness on such a hot day.'

'My very sincere thanks to both of you then, since I really do not want to arrive back at my friend's house in a shift or a sack and I would roast in your cloak by the time we got to Broadley as well as looking like a figure of fun. I promise I will take great care of your sister's good gown and I am sure that my friend Miss Donne will stand over her long-suffering maid and see that it is laundered very carefully indeed before we return it. I am sorry your father had to give up his living, by the way.'

'So is he; my parents were very well suited to their busy lives at the centre of a wide parish, but they do not go on half so well now they have not got much to do or much of a pension to do it with. It seems that middling folk who go to live in Bath for the benefit of their health must amuse themselves with gossip, tea drinking and taking the waters if they are not to be run off their feet and land in the sponging house. Mama seems to have taken to it all like a duck to water, but I know my father misses his parishioners and our rambling old vicarage as well as his study full of books and the pupils he used to take in to supplement his income.'

'Idleness can seem far harder to endure than being too busy at times,' Fliss said. Her own doubts about her new life, if she did not marry and have Lord Stratford's heirs and spares to keep her occupied, resurfaced. But never mind her personal dilemmas, Marianne must have felt even more grief stricken for her husband once she was back with her parents and living such a confined life, especially since her mother and father had not approved of her choice of a husband in the first place.

'That sounds like the voice of experience,' Marianne said lightly.

Fliss concluded she did not want to talk about that dark time in her life now she was busy again and from the state of this old house looked as if she would be so for a very long time. 'Perhaps, although I doubt I was as busy as you are here. I am having a holiday from being a governess. I am between positions and it feels very odd not to be busy teaching my former pupil or planning lessons and activities to keep such an acute young lady out of mischief,' she said with a shrug and felt guilty about hiding her good fortune from most of the world. She had resolved to keep it secret until she was certain what she wanted to do about Lord Stratford's proposal, since news of her inheritance would attract fortune hunters and she was not quite free to be courted by anyone until she had given him an answer one way or the other.

Chapter Five

'I should be grateful for the respite and remember how much I used to long for even half a day to myself when I was responsible for my last pupil most of our waking hours,' Fliss said ruefully. 'I miss teaching far more than I expected to when I promised my own former governess I would stay with her for the rest of the spring and most of the summer when I got here at the beginning of June.'

'Your pupil did not have any family willing or able to care for her so you could have a few hours to yourself, then?' Marianne asked, shaking her head at what she took for wilful neglect. It was true that Juno and her grandmother had very little in common, so maybe she was right. The Dowager had scarcely seen her orphaned granddaughter until she was of an age to marry off, which was probably why she had scoffed at Fliss's suggestion it might be best to bring Juno out in local society first. 'I am sorry to seem as if I am criticising you when I admire you for caring for the girl you were there to teach, as well as making her into a proper young lady, but I do dislike this habit aristocratic families have of handing over their girls to strangers until they are old enough to marry and taking very little notice of them in the meantime.'

'I might have to agree with you if I was not one of those strangers you are talking about, but the girl's grandmother is such an exacting and impatient lady I am glad she did not trouble herself much with Juno until recently. She seems to believe the poor girl could stop being so shy if she would only apply herself and Juno's uncle and guardian is unwed so she could not live with him. I suppose Juno and I grew to rely on one another for company and she is a bright and amusing girl under her diffidence with strangers and I never could get her to overcome that however hard I tried.'

'You sound as if you grew very fond of her, so you must miss her now she is supposed to be grown up and no longer in need of a governess.'

'Yes, and I worry about her so, Marianne. I think she needed to have a much quieter debut so she could gradually get used to knowing more people and learn to judge who is kind and who might be cruel before being pushed into the wider world. Instead of that she has had to endure the grand fuss of being a debutante and her presentation at Court and it has not gone well. As a governess I had no influence over her future and her grandmother was impatient to get her off her hands.'

Fliss knew that if she wed Lord Stratford the Dowager could not run the poor girl's life any more, though, because she would. If she had only agreed to an engagement before he went away she could be with Juno in London as her future aunt by marriage at this very moment. Even the Dowager would have to listen to the views of her future daughter-in-law, with Lord Stratford's steely wrath to look forward to if she haughtily ignored the former governess who had had the gall to agree to be his wife, even if she *was* Lord Netherton's niece and almost well bred. As long as you ignored that unfortunate connection to the navy, of course, and Fliss doubted the Dowager Viscountess Stratford would ever truly be able to do that.

'Being so painfully shy must be a curse to a girl of high enough rank to be presented at Court and her grandmother does not sound at all sympathetic.'

'I did not equip her well enough for the life she must lead,' Fliss said, feeling as if she had failed Juno in that as well as not immediately agreeing to wed her guardian and save her the misery of her debut Season. 'If only I had got her out of her shell and persuaded her to make friends with the young people in her local area she would be much happier now. At the very least I should have made more effort to get her grandmother to see how very shy she is and warned her guardian more strongly that she was not ready for such a public debut as well.'

'It sounds as if the lady would have dismissed you for arguing and the gentleman is too busy to take much notice, so I cannot see how it all became your fault the girl has such selfish and inconsiderate relatives who care more about what they want than what is good for her.'

That was not quite fair to Lord Stratford, but a good enough reading of the haughty Dowager. Fliss still felt torn by choices Marianne did not know about, though, and she could hardly tell her without betraying secrets that were not entirely her own to tell. 'Maybe they are not as bad as I paint them,' she said lightly and gestured at the muddy and soap-scum-laden water, 'but how is this bath going to be emptied, scrubbed out and got ready for your use when it is in such a dreadful state? I can hardly help you bail it out and carry out the dirty water in nothing but a shift.'

'Don't worry, Jenks, our handyman, is making me a henhouse in one of the barns so he can help me. You had better hide in Viola's bedchamber while I harry him and anyone else I can find to get the next bath organised.'

'The water will barely be lukewarm by now,' Fliss objected as she followed her new friend upstairs.

'Luckily it is a fine day and I am far too warm for comfort already, so I will be glad if it is cool and I do not have quite as much dirt to get rid of as you did,' Marianne said as she led Fliss across the wide panelled hall and up a fine oak staircase that must have been carved to impress visitors several centuries ago. 'I insisted on having the hall and landing clean and fit to walk on as soon as the kitchen was ready to cook and eat in again,' Marianne told her as if Fliss might be worried about getting dust or dirt on her bare feet after what they had been through this morning.

'It is a fine old house,' she said sincerely and admired the leaded windows that were letting light on to the stairs and all the loving details the family who built this place had put into their grand new creation. 'It has a good feel about it,' she added truthfully, 'and if you have any ghosts they feel like friendly ones.'

'Aye, if we have they have never done us any harm. Maybe they are too grateful that the dust of ages is finally being swept from their ancestral hall to haunt us,' Marianne replied and unlatched an ancient oak door on the wide landing and ushered Fliss inside.

'Oh, this is such a lovely room!' Fliss exclaimed. The large bedchamber was as fresh and fine as hard work and ancient craftsmanship could make it. There were two delicately leaded windows looking out at the miniature lake on one side and up the valley on the other one. It felt as if it had all been designed with love and her friend had lavished a lot more on it as she cleared and cleaned it. It seemed she had found all the best things left in the house to welcome her little sister to her new home, if Miss Yelverton was ever free to spend time at Owlet Manor between the demands of her employers and her duty to her parents in distant Bath.

'It is rather old fashioned and threadbare,' Marianne argued with a wry shrug.

'No, it is mellow and peaceful and welcoming and I can just imagine a long-ago daughter of the house being so proud of having her own fine room once upon a time that she might come back and haunt anyone who does not love it as dearly as she must have done.'

'And you have far too much imagination to spend very long in such an old house without making up a family from long ago to haunt it for you.'

'Don't,' Fliss said with a shudder for her nine-year-old self plagued by nightmares of her stiff-necked and angry ancestors scolding her in the ancient stone passages and echoing halls of Netherton Park as she tried to adjust to a bleak life without her parents in it. 'This house feels like a happy home, not a lord's stronghold with a guilty secret around every corner.'

'It does and I love it far too much already,' Marianne said. 'Now give me that wet towel and put this one around your shoulders while I fetch you a comb. You can unknot that wild mane of yours while I chivvy the men into doing my bidding downstairs. I dare say in this heat your hair will almost be dry by the time I am done so we can pin it up and make you respectable again for the journey back to Broadley.'

Fliss meekly thanked her new friend and found the long and knotty problem of carefully teasing the tangles out of her long hair dreamy and almost sooth-ing in this lovely old bedchamber, until she came up against a stubborn one and had to concentrate on getting it freed without having to ask for some scis-sors to cut through the knotted mess. As well if she had less time to wonder how it would feel to wander about in a warm and intimate bedchamber like this one, languidly performing such tasks with a sated lover lazily watching every move she made as if she fascinated him. Would he rise from their bed and take the comb, trying to gently soothe the knots out for her, since he was the one who helped her make them in the first place? Or would he be diverted from the task at hand by the feel and smoothness of her silky curls under his fingers and the silken snare of her fine skin under a soft lawn or silk chemise? Instead of acting the lady's maid for her, would he turn her around and look deep into her eyes with a sensual question in his light blue ones? Know-ing the answer would be, *yes*, she would return that look with a heady invitation to seduce her all over again, to show her why it was a good idea for them to linger up here wasting good daylight, when there was so much still to do on his rundown farm and his almost-lost-in-time house and garden. They would waste time so beautifully it would feel as if they had twice the energy when they remembered who they were again and what they still had to do to make this old house as perfect as they ever wanted it to be. Her hand slowed and her eyelids grew heavy; her lips parted as if they had been kissed into lush opulence by a lover who... Who did not look in the least bit like Lord Stratford and that would never do!

Tossing the comb aside, Fliss began to pace the carefully cleaned and restored-to-order bedchamber. This would simply not do. She was too involved with another man to have such sinful thoughts about Mr Darius Yelverton, even if he wanted her to. She caught sight of herself padding about the room wearing not very much at all in the watery old mirror she somehow knew Marianne had saved for her sister rather than hoarding it for her own use. She was touched by such sisterly love, even as she was distracted by the image of herself in it, a more vivid and vital version of herself than she had ever seen before. This was not the Miss Grantham who had set out this morning for a short stroll in the countryside to compose herself and think hard about the future after yet another mournful letter from her former pupil. Nor was it the cool and self-contained lady who had managed to face Lord Stratford with serenity when he made her that unexpected offer of marriage on the last day she would ever spend at his mother's Dower House as Juno's governess. Her cheeks were flushed now and she was ashamed it was not because of the warmth of the weather, but the heat of her fantasies about a very different man alto-gether. Her fiery curls were loose about her shoulders and looking silky and lover-tempting now, but they were the same curls she had this morning when she pinned them severely into place for a sedate walk on the edge of the town. There was something about the face they surrounded that made them look new and different as well, because she *felt* new and different, inside and out. And she should not. Mr Yelverton's intent light blue gaze had woken something inside her that ought to stay asleep and unaware, until her husband woke it up on their wedding night. Except she could not envisage Lord Stratford at all as she stood here dreaming of another man, let alone see him as the wonderfully suitable husband who would perform such a wonder on that night. Especially as they had been so indifferent to one another as po-tential lovers for the last four years and he was such an aloof gentleman she could not even imagine him as an impassioned lover, let alone hers.

Ah, and wasn't that the truth of the whole matter? She and Lord Stratford *were* more or less indiffer-ent to one another as anything but potential friends, now they were a lot more equal than they used to be. They would be foolish to press an almost friend-ship into a second-best sort of a marriage. So she had an answer to one of her dilemmas at long last. Mr Darius Yelverton would be surprised to know he had helped her discover one course she would not be taking through life, at Lord Stratford's side.

He would be surprised and a little bit disturbed in case she had latched on to him as her potential husband instead as well, she suspected. He would see her as unsuitable and poor—but then so was he. So that was that. She would demand equality of effort in any marriage she was ever tempted to enter from now on and Darius Yelverton's heart would not be in it, so she should have no more of that potent fantasy.

She stopped pacing the wide and ancient oak floorboards and confronted her reflection again almost like an enemy. The girl in there looked a bit wild, a touch untrustworthy and far too capable of deep feelings and unrestrained passions of all sorts that the real Fliss had not even dreamt existed when she got up this morning to a perfectly blue sky and beckoning countryside. New Fliss looked dangerous and silly to the old one and it was high time she reintroduced reason and order. First she would search through the hairpins and lengths of ribbon the younger sister must have given to Marianne for safe keeping, as well as her best gowns, so she could find a way to control her witchy locks and get that wild and yearning Fliss under control again. At least she had the means to replace anything she used now and Miss Grantham's deft fingers ruthlessly wound her rebellious curls into stern order. Fliss pinned the last one firmly in place and faced herself in the mirror with a severe nod to tell the girl in there she had better not contrast this coolly contained hairstyle and carefully impassive features with the transparent old cotton shift that barely covered her generous curves and left most of her as bare as the day she was born. Her legs were bruised, she noted when she slid her glance from the still defiantly aware face of the hussy in the mirror to examine the bits of herself she could not see in it. The marks of her graceless fall into the mud were already darkening her pale skin and she would probably be black and blue all over come the morning.

'Here you are; I knew I had put these aside to think about later,' Marianne told her after a cursory knock at the door to warn Fliss she was back. 'They might fit you well enough not to fall off, even if they will look odd in this century. Probably not as odd as you going home barefoot would, though, and I am quite sure you would not want to put your own shoes back on until they have had a very thorough clean, if we can ever manage to get them clean again and not smelling like a murky pond, which I doubt.'

'Goodness,' said Fliss, staring at the much embroidered and high-heeled satin shoes Marianne was holding out to her like a trophy. 'Are you sure? They must have been very fine once upon a time and have hardly even been worn, but they look as if they ought to be kept in a cabinet of curiosities now.'

'If you can walk in them, then you are very welcome to wear them. I doubt such ridiculous fashions will ever come back and only imagine how ridiculous I would look three inches above where I am now, towering above all and sundry as I pick my way round the farmyard, even if I could cram them on my feet in the first place.'

Marianne laughed at the very idea and Fliss caught a glimpse of the light-hearted and indomitable lady she must have been when her husband was alive. How terribly it must have hurt to lose the love of her life like that and Fliss was almost glad she had never found hers as she considered the tearing pain of losing him.

'Whereas I could do with a few extra inches,' she joked to stop her new friend thinking the same thing and slipped her feet into the strange old shoes to see if they would fit. 'Ooh, I *like* it up here,' she said as she stood up experimentally and took a few wobbly steps, but it was true.

It was hard to be a little dab of a thing when your ordinary shoes or kid slippers had not even the hint of a heel to change your perspective. Now she was on the same level as most other people it gave her a new idea of the world and maybe she would be able to hold a conversation with certain so-called gentlemen without them addressing her bosom throughout it. She thought about the brutish glint in certain male gazes and decided they probably did it to every youngish lady they came across, irrespective of how tall or short they might be. Still, it would be nice not to feel so small and vulnerable in such company and she would welcome a return to such fanciful footwear if it could do that for the likes of her and an oh-so-accidental stamp of these heels on a handy male foot might make them stand a little further away as well.

'Now we have you shod, I think you must try Viola's figured muslin on next and hope it will not sweep the floor now you have an extra few inches to buoy you up,' Marianne said practically and tossed the gown over Fliss's head before she could argue.

Luckily it was the right length now Fliss was three inches higher up, although the high bodice would have been strained to the edge of indecency if they could only do it up. After a few moments struggling with the laces they decided they must stay loose for fear of tearing the fine fabric if they tried to do them up one more time. It was not the right day to wear more than was strictly necessary, but Marianne fetched a delicate white-work shawl from her own room and Fliss guessed she had made it herself. Poor Marianne; she must have been very bored indeed while she was living in Bath to have found enough patience for such delicate and meticulous embroidery.

Once the shawl was pinned like a fichu and a sash tied under her bosom to stop the gown gaping at least Fliss was respectable again with its help and, as Marianne said, the shadows cast by Miss Viola Yelverton's parasol would hide even more of her from prying eyes. Apparently the sturdy farm horse would only walk in the afternoon heat so there was no risk of it being snatched out of Fliss's hand by their speed. She hoped Marianne would take the middle seat in the gig, since several miles of being pressed hard against Mr Yelverton's firmly muscled body with all these wicked thoughts milling about in her head was enough to make Fliss blush even thinking about it.

'I sent a lad to Broadley on the other horse with a note for your friend, Miss Donne, to tell her where you are and when you and her dog should be home. As the lad is small and light he will be able to take a few shortcuts so the letter ought to get to her well before us. I hope it will reassure her all is well,' Mr Yelverton told Fliss stiffly when they met in the kitchen some time later.

Marianne had brought Fliss up a light luncheon and a very welcome mug of tea so she was well out of the way when her brother took his bath, in what must have been cold water since Luna had been bathed in Marianne's lukewarm one and she had been nearly as muddy as Fliss and perhaps even more smelly after rolling in who wanted to know what. He was very clean and gentlemanly now and she missed the work-mussed and impatient Darius the Farmer in this very correct Squire Yelverton. She must not call him Darius though, must she? Not even in her head. Mr Yelverton looked stiff and uncomfortable in his Sunday best, but he was still a fine and well-set-up gentleman and what on earth was the matter with her? Lord Stratford's beautifully tailored clothes and carelessly elegant air of distinction had never aroused this dangerous shiver at the very heart of her. The thought of this man in scarlet regimentals, a sword at his side and generally polished up in full regimental fig was one fantasy too many as well. She made herself turn away so she could fuss over Luna while the acute little creature decided whether or not she ought to take a dislike to the patient carriage horse that was waiting for them all to get on with whatever it was it had been harnessed to do.

The gig looked far too small to seat three adult human beings even to the end of their drive, let alone however many miles it was from here to Broadley. Fliss was wondering how she would survive jammed up against Mr Yelverton's hard-muscled and very masculine body without giving herself away as a wanton who ought to be ashamed of herself when Marianne reappeared wearing a plain dark gown and a fine straw bonnet that was tied very firmly in place. She also wore supple leather gloves that must feel far too warm on such a sultry day and Fliss supposed she should not be surprised when Mr Yelverton handed his sister up into the driving seat, helped Fliss to climb up the other side with cool efficiency, then strode off in the direction of the stables, but she still was. He obviously did not want to endure the enforced intimacy of a carriage ride with her pressed so close against his body either and why on earth did that make her feel rejected?

'Don't worry, I will not overturn us,' Marianne said with a grin and Fliss really hoped she could not read her mind. She wished she had no idea what was going on in there herself at the moment.

'I never thought you would,' she managed to say calmly enough and of course she was not disappointed, that would be quite ridiculous.

'But you are still surprised I am the one who will be doing the driving today, I dare say. My brother is such a gallant soul he often gets me to do so even when he does deign to join me in the gig, mainly because he knows I am the better driver. I am ready to admit to you, although I shall deny it strenuously if I ever meet the local gentry, that I got used to riding astride in Portugal and Spain. I have never quite got used to being properly ladylike in a side saddle again and, since I have far more experience of driving carts than my brother, I prefer to drive rather than wobble about in a ladylike fashion on top of a horse. I was a sergeant's wife and Darius was one of the officers so he could not lower himself to take the reins when we were on the march,' Marianne told her lightly.

Fliss suspected an old soreness between brother and sister at the change of status Marianne must have undergone as a soldier's wife. Marianne must have been brought up to take it for granted she was gentry and had more privileges than most of their neighbours. Yet she seemed cheerful and a bit nostalgic about the privations of life on the march in the tail of a large army and, Fliss supposed, with enough love to sweeten the hardship, anything was possible and maybe even necessary to stay with the one you loved. She wondered if she would have had the resolution and passion and sheer faith in another human being to love her back, come what may, and admired Marianne all the more for following her heart instead of her head.

'Are you putting thoughts in my head again, Sister dear?' Mr Yelverton asked from the other side of the stable yard.

Fliss slewed around in her seat to stare like a yokel as he rode towards them on a magnificent and currently very restless horse. It was not quite a thoroughbred, but that was probably just as well if it had been on campaign. It would need stamina as well as spirit and courage for such long rides through challenging countryside. The animal was beautifully put together, whatever its breeding, and it looked as if it could go all day. They made a striking pair, the fighting fit masculine rider holding his spirited and powerful horse to a sort of stillness contained with an effort, as if it was an overwound spring on the verge of breaking free. She could imagine the two of them on the edge of battle, lined up ahead of his men and eager to have this over and done with and an end to waiting. No, infantry officers walked with their men rather than riding ahead of them, didn't they? Whatever they did, she sensed Mr Yelverton must have been in two minds about the whole bloody business as he waited to kill or be killed yet again. His horse looked almost fierce enough to fight for him as it snorted and pawed the ground now and reminded her of accounts she had read of warhorses trained to actively fight off attackers in ancient battles between armoured knights. The animal looked as if it would bite or kick anyone who dared threaten his master, then or now.

'Goodness,' she said. 'What a noble-looking animal.'

'He is, although I fear Nero's manners do not always live up to his looks,' he said with an affectionate pat for the jigging animal as it tried to turn and nip playfully at its rider's legs and he laughed and controlled it with almost insulting ease. She thought it looked like a playful move rather than a grab for power in their ongoing battle of wills, but with teeth like those who could say for certain?

'Nero will not allow anyone but my brother to ride him, which is why the great sentimental idiot has a warhorse eating his head off in the stables rather than selling him and using the money to buy something tame and a lot more use on the farm,' Marianne said with a mock-severe look for her brother.

'Several somethings, I expect,' he said mildly and actually laughed when his sentimental attachment tried to buck him off half-seriously. Fliss's heart was in her mouth at the thought of him being thrown against one of the solid walls around the stable yard. 'Although I have to agree that he is in desperate need of a good run,' he added as if he was almost apologising for the fact that he was about to leave them to their own devices while he rode some of the fidgets out of his restless horse.

Fliss decided she would prefer him to be an arrogant and impatient man to go with his arrogant and impatient horse. That might stop her appreciating the sight of so much muscular male strength in motion, the man lithe and easy in the saddle and looking like a spinster's fantasy lover, the mighty horse barely contained by his powerful rider and eager for action.

'Do not let us stop you, Darius. I suppose you will have had time to get to Broadley and back before we are even halfway there,' Marianne answered calmly, apparently oblivious to the effect her brother was having on Fliss. He had probably dazzled dozens of females in Portugal, Spain and France and wherever else he had been in his scarlet coat and all the other unfair details of his dashing uniform.

'Then if *you* will excuse me, Miss Grantham?'

He asked that polite question as if she was a formal acquaintance. She felt put in her place as she agreed stiffly to do so. He raised his hat while holding the spirited animal steady by the strength of those long and sleekly muscular legs that really did show to advantage in gentlemanly riding dress, so she had been right about that much at least.

Marianne shook the reins and clicked her tongue at her patient horse to set it in motion and her brother made his restless mount trot by their side as meekly as a child's pony until they were all safely out of the yard. He rode at Fliss's side of the little carriage as they passed the farm buildings, and she could see the effort it took him to keep the animal to such a slow pace. Through those skin-tight riding breeches she could see the play of his impressive muscles and she blushed under the shade of her borrowed parasol and berated herself for finding him so male and appealing and hoped he had no idea she was not the proper governess he seemed to think her. He gave her a wry smile, put the head of his riding crop to his hat in a gesture of farewell then horse and rider peeled away from the gig once they were clear of the last barn and out of the double iron gates that looked as if they had not been closed this century and most of the one before. His horse went up the gentle slope in a bound and was out and on to the unfenced grassland in the blink of an eye. Fliss could see far enough from her seat in the gig to watch them shift from trot to a smooth canter before they were out of sight over the first hedge and the slope downhill beyond it.

She had to stop staring at the empty space where he had been, before his sister noticed her silly fascination with Farmer Yelverton's broad shoulders and narrow waist as he moved with his fine horse as lithely as a jockey and either frowned or smiled, depending on her opinion of Miss Felicity Grantham as a prospective sister-in-law. And wasn't that a ridiculous idea?

'The sheep are used to them by now,' Marianne said as if Fliss might be worried about the flock she could hear nearby now she was not quite as distracted.

It had not even occurred to her to fear the stock might prove a stumbling block to his headlong progress, nor had she been able to think about anything much past this ridiculously raw yearning for a man she had only met a couple of hours ago as she watched him ride over the horizon. She really could not understand herself; she was nearly an engaged woman, for goodness sake, or at the very least she owed Lord Stratford a, *No, thank you,* before she started yearning for another man. What a shame a lady could not correspond with a gentleman who was not closely related to her, so she was unable to write to His Lordship and explain that she really could not marry him. She would leave out the large and too compellingly masculine reason she had woken up to that fact before they risked lifetime tied to one another by the fragile thread of a maybe friendship and concern for Juno's well-being.

And Darius Yelverton clearly had a reckless spirit if he thought dashing about the country on such a wild and headlong animal was as much fun as it looked when he sat poised on his horse before he was lost to sight. It was as if he understood every ridiculous male impulse his mount wanted to give full rein to and what a great joke life was. The man was obviously hiding a very different soul under all the gentlemanly reserve he had fooled her with when he led the way from that untidy woodland to his rundown new home, with her meekly trotting behind. There was no sign of the quiet and restrained countryman in that wild man galloping across the downs like a centaur. The wild part of her that had once loved sailing ahead of the wind; glorying in the forces of nature even when they posed dangers she had refused to think of when her parents were still alive, agreed it looked like a wonderful, exhilarating sort of freedom to be able to ride like that. One more thing they did not have in common then; one more reason for her to go back to Miss Donne's house and forget her encounter with a man who would probably have a hard time recalling her name by this time tomorrow. He certainly would not have a very good impression of what she looked like after their disastrous first meeting even if he did recall her when they next met. Lord Stratford would have been a much safer bet to yearn for, so what a shame she could not languish over him instead. She did not think he would like it even if she did, so it was doubly as well she had decided it would not do to marry him and hope love and respect would grow between them as they built a life and a family together.

Once she was back in the little town house Miss Donne had made so neat and comfortable the events of the day would fall back into place. She had suffered a ridiculous and embarrassing mishap and endured a great deal of anxiety, thanks to Luna's dash for freedom. By tomorrow she would have her usual practical common-sense approach to life firmly back in place. She would be immune to his charm and his handsome face, his lithe body and former career as an officer in hard-fought battles through Portugal, Spain and France. Yet he could easily have handed her the dog and walked away with a few gruff directions back to Broadley, never mind the state she was in. He had far more important things to do than rescue damsels in distress, but he put them aside and escorted her back to his home.

When they got to Broadley she must thank him for his kindness and learn to see him as he really was, though. He was stubborn, quixotic and probably a rake at heart if that dare-the-devil look he gave her before he galloped off was anything to go by. If the state of his house and land was a true indication of his finances, he would need to marry money if he was ever to get it all back in good order and it certainly wasn't going to be her fortune that put his land and his house to rights. A besotted woman might hand over all she had and all she was to such a fine-looking man, never mind mutual love, or respect, or even a mild sort of liking on his side. It was a very good thing she had asked Miss Donne to keep her new wealth secret until she knew what she really wanted to do with her life. She hated the idea of being courted for her newly acquired fortune, especially by a fortune hunter who looked like him.

Chapter Six

'Oh, my dear girl, what a shocking thing to have happened before you have even had enough time to learn the lie of the land around here and summon help and it sounds as if it was all your fault, you *naughty* little dog,' Miss Donne exclaimed once she had been introduced to Fliss's rescuers and heard about her misadventure in more detail.

The dog, who had sat meekly in Fliss's lap all the way here as if she was a born lapdog and would never dream of running away, flattened her ears against her neat little skull and wagged her stubby little tail at her beloved mistress. Even Fliss would have to admit Luna looked appealing and almost innocent, if you didn't know better. 'She is completely shameless,' she said severely, all too conscious of Mr Yelverton sitting on his horse behind the little carriage now said horse was pretending to be as calm as a fat pony after its dash over the hills and far away. She wondered if they had got as far as the Welsh border while she and Marianne were plodding the dusty roads that wandered around the hills and valleys as if they had all the time in the world to get here. Probably not, but they had certainly got here more directly than the steady little carriage could when he finally deigned to join them again on their last stretch of the journey into town. She wished she had a bird's-eye view of them tearing about the countryside in their dashing glory while they rode the devil out of themselves mile after mile.

Remembering how shrewd her old friend was, Fliss did her best to block such improper thoughts as she introduced her rescuers to Miss Donne. The lady had clearly summed the brother and sister up as proper gentry and invited them to step inside and take tea with them, or maybe a glass of ale in Mr Yelverton's case, so they could quench their thirst after such a hot and dusty journey.

'The King's Head have excellent stabling and will look after that fine animal of yours and your carriage horse until you are ready to go home again,' Miss Donne told them briskly. 'You have been kind to my dear friend and I would like to say a proper thank you and become better acquainted with you both as well.'

'Very well then, I must admit a drink and a few moments to sit in the shade in peace before we must return home in this heat sounds very welcome,' Marianne answered for both of them.

Fliss thought from the careful blankness of her

brother's expression that he would rather take his ale
at the inn and ride back as fast as possible. He ought
to think of his sister's reputation and safety as she
drove home. Local society would be all too ready to
find fault with a lady who had been careless enough
of her station to marry a common soldier if he did not
have a little more care for Marianne's status among
them than Marianne probably wanted him to. Anyway, he agreed to Miss Donne's plan after his sister's eager reply and they drove and rode away to
stable the horses.

'Now we will have just enough time to get you
out of that borrowed gown and those peculiar shoes
and into your own clothes again before they arrive
back here, Felicity. You will feel better in your own
clothes after your misadventure,' Miss Donne said
as she urged Fliss inside.

'I would certainly be glad not to have to risk
bursting out of Miss Yelverton's best gown in public any longer,' Fliss replied ruefully. 'The fabric
has stood up to the strain quite admirably thus far,
but I am such a dumpy little creature it is unlikely
I would chance across just such another to borrow
gowns. Mrs Turner's gowns would have been quite
impossible, but even with all these pins to keep this
scarf in place it is a risk to wear it for any longer
than I must.'

'Indeed, although it sounds as if your own gown
was quite ruined, along with everything else you had
on and they could hardly bring you back wrapped

in a sack. And don't worry, I will watch Bet like a hawk when she launders this gown so we can send it back good as new, but do come upstairs now and get into your own clothes before those two return and we are not ready to greet them.'

'I am quite grown up, you know? I can get dressed on my own and quite often do so,' Fliss protested.

'I know you; you will take so long about it that you will miss saying farewell and another thank you to your kind rescuers simply because you are so embarrassed that Mr Yelverton chanced upon you in such a predicament. You cannot skulk upstairs feeling sorry for yourself when good manners demand so much more from you and so do I.'

'Yes, Miss Donne; certainly, Miss Donne; whatever you say, Miss Donne.'

'Impudent girl,' her friend said placidly.

Fliss decided there was no point in trying to assert herself as a grown up woman of four and twenty when Miss Donne was in full governess mode like this. And for some silly reason it seemed important to be dressed well when the brother and sister came back. She had to sympathise with Miss Yelverton's reasons for leaving this gown with her sister for safe keeping while Miss Donne set about the task of carefully stripping it off with as little damage as possible. If Miss Yelverton wore this finely embroidered gown to take her charges down to the drawing room one day, or to a local dance if she happened to be invited for some unexpected reason,

the work and fineness of it would tell her employers
that she had a life beyond them, beyond being their
meek and largely unseen governess, and that might
make their whole situation a little too real for comfort. Both Fliss and Miss Yelverton had been born
gentlemen's daughters and not as teachers in miniature, so why did the world insist a governess was
an upper servant, confined to a schoolroom with
her pupils all day and set apart from them only at
night? Once she had crossed their threshold as ed-
ucator and mentor of their daughters, a household
appeared to think of the governess as a colourless
automaton who would only speak when spoken to.
So Fliss knew this was more than a fine gown to its
owner—it was a holiday from being plain and properly humble whenever her employers laid eyes on her.
Dressed in this finely made and very pretty gown she
could be Miss Yelverton again, a gentleman's daughter and, if her brother and sister were anything to go
by, an attractive and adventurous young woman in
her own right. Knowing what her best gowns meant
to a fellow governess who was not yet old enough to
be thought of as at her last prayers, Fliss kept very
still while her friend removed the pins Marianne had
used to make the soft shawl cover her modesty. She
breathed a sigh of relief when gown and shawl were
finally free and there were no great pinholes or tears
in either. At least now she could breathe out properly for the first time since she had put these clothes

on in Viola Yelverton's touchingly beautiful and yet starkly empty bedroom.

'What a very fine piece of white work this is. Mrs Turner has every right to feel proud of her skill with a needle,' Miss Donne said as she draped the shawl gently over the back of a chair.

Fliss carefully shrugged out of the fine gown and laid that aside for Miss Donne's long-suffering maid to inspect for damage and launder and iron so it could go back to Owlet Manor in perfect order.

'Mrs Turner has told me Miss Yelverton taught at Miss Thibett's Academy for Young Ladies in Bath before she became a governess to her present pupils,' she remarked in the hope of diverting Miss Donne from her own shortcomings as a needlewoman.

'A very fine school it is as well, but the younger lady must be quieter and a little more conventional than her elder sister if she was employed as a mistress there for very long.'

'Mrs Turner is a lady to her fingertips,' Fliss defended her new friend hotly and Miss Donne raised her eyebrows. 'I like her,' she added with a shrug. 'She is capable and kind and I find it very hard to care whom she married when her husband must have been a very fine man for her to make such a drastic change in her life for his sake, then follow him to war and endure daily hardship and constant anxiety for his safety while they lived together on campaign.'

'Even upon a very short acquaintance Mrs Turner does not strike me as the sort of female to meekly wait around for a more suitable marriage than the one she did make, or the kind to fit easily into a narrow life as a spinster daughter because her chosen partner in life seemed like too much of a risk for her to marry. Better for her to find love with an ordinary man than run away with an exciting rogue out of sheer boredom and she looks the sort of girl who would be very bored with nothing much to do,' Miss Donne said—she had learnt a lot about Marianne in a very short time. Fliss hoped her shrewd mentor was not quite as shrewd about Mr Yelverton as she had been about his sister, or she might already have some wrongheaded ideas about how Fliss felt about him.

'You will not mind if I elope with the handyman, then?' she joked lightly to divert her.

'Of course I will; you would not suit one another at all.'

At least the notion of Fliss going all the way to Gretna Green with the gruff and mostly silent middle-aged man who was employed by several of the local ladies for his skills with a screwdriver and a hammer, if not his silver tongue, made them both laugh. It helped unwind some of the tension Fliss had felt knotting ever tighter inside her since the first moment she laid eyes on Mr Yelverton and had to contrast her own muddied and stinking person with his work-mussed and lightly perspiring one. He would never get that first impression of her out of his mind now and that hurt for some reason she refused to think about.

She shooed Miss Donne out of the room once she was down to the ancient shift again. Alone at last, she removed that final layer of strangeness with a sigh and eyed her naked figure in the mirror. There was no real change in it since this morning. She did have bruises beginning to show on her pale skin and the odd graze and a fine scratch from the brambles in Mr Yelverton's wild wood. Plus her palms ached from the impact when she had tripped and they had taken most of the weight of her falling body until she collapsed into the mud, but all that would pass and she would look much the same when she had some clothes on. Thank heavens there was not as much as a grain of mud left on her though. She wrinkled her nose at the memory of being covered in the stuff more or less from head to toe and sighed once again.

She glanced critically at her image in the mirror and wished she was longer in the leg and less well endowed in the bosom. A few inches' difference here and there might make her elegant and unforgettable with nothing on instead of short and… well…dumpy and not very elegant at all as well as currently rather bruised and battered. Unfortunately there did not seem any other word she could use to describe herself but dumpy. And Mr Yelverton was a tall and rather elegantly made man, so they would be ill matched in every way she could think of if there was ever the slightest chance of them being matched like this at all. It might be as well if she stopped thinking about him now, especially when she was as undressed as this and the very thought of him in the same state of nature was waking up those wicked fantasies again.

'You still have four good limbs and are in possession of all your senses, Felicity, so just be grateful for such blessings,' she chided herself and turned away from the disappointing sight of herself naked. She was not at all the sort of female men wrote sonnets to or carried an image of away in their hearts when they left on a quest to prove their everlasting devotion, or worthiness for her hand in marriage, and that was that. She was squat and plain and had red hair; add the new batch of freckles after her walk in the sun without a hat and it was no wonder Mr Yelverton walked ahead of her all the way back to his house to save himself the ordeal of looking at her. The wonder was he had not left her where she was while he went home to fetch a farm cart, then threw her out of it into the nearest pond and had her brought home by his carter unkempt and stinking and still wet.

'Good, you look much more like your usual self,' Miss Donne said when Fliss finally came down the fine oak stairs of her hostess's not-particularly-simple cottage as her old and neatly contained self, even if she didn't feel much like the composed young woman who had come down them first thing this morning.

She had brushed her hair again and pinned it into a neat chignon and dressed herself very neatly in the hope of overpainting Mr Yelverton and Marianne's first impressions of her with a much better and tidier one. She also added a few drops of lavender oil here and there to ward off any last hint of the smell of stagnant mud that might be lingering about her person. A careful sniff of every part of her she could reach before she dressed again proved Marianne's homemade washing ball had been very effective at removing it from her skin and hair, even if her senses could not quite get rid of the memory of the stench as she made her way back to Owlet Manor in Darius Yelverton's wake.

'And I do like that particular shade of yellow with your lovely hair,' Marianne said impulsively as if she truly admired her horrid hair and the lemon-yellow summer gown Fliss had chosen as a small rebellion against being a seen-and-not-heard servant last summer *and* in defiance of the dressmaker's disapproving comment that it would make her hair look even brighter. It was none of the seamstress's business how the Stratfords' governess chose to dress, but Fliss had never found the courage to wear the light and colourful gown at the Dower House. Instead she had imagined the Dowager's shocked expression if she had put off her usual greys and dark, unseen colours and quailed, so it had been kept in a cupboard ever since it came back from the dressmaker.

So what did that say about such small, but costly, rebellions? That they were usually wasted on those they were intended to startle, she supposed. Another lesson learned then, but it did feel rather wonderful not to dress in grey or fade-into-the-furniture mud colours now she no longer had to work for her living. Mr Yelverton was not likely to be impressed by her looks or her gown after that first terrible impression anyway, but she had her pride and it made her want to show him she was not quite the disaster he must have thought her when they met in the wood.

'Yes, indeed, very becoming,' he said solemnly now and bowed to her as if she was at least Miss Donne's age to take the edge off his compliment.

'Here is your tea, my love,' Miss Donne said with a sympathetic smile that said Fliss might be in need of some after such lacklustre praise.

'Thank you,' Fliss replied and wished she could kiss her old friend for always being such a strong support to her when her insecurities threatened. If only she had managed to bring Juno out of her paralysing shyness, she would feel more effective as a governess and she was reminded how hard it had been to walk away from a sobbing Juno on that awful last day at the Dower House. She pushed the memory to the back of her mind lest she cry herself.

'Ah, that is quite delicious,' she said with a sigh of content. It washed the dust of the roads out of her throat and the familiar scent of best China tea took her back to childhood birthday and Christmas meals with her governess. Lord Netherton and the family usually managed to ignore the two cuckoos in their nest at such times, so Fliss and Miss Donne used to treat themselves to a few secretive luxuries and celebrate in private. Yes, she was a lucky woman and there was no use wishing she had a close family like Marianne's. Well, perhaps her parents sounded rather less than doting after her rebellion and marriage to her Daniel, but the three siblings were obviously close. Their careful preparations for Miss Yelverton's reception if she ever managed to get away from her employment spoke of deep love. Her room had been put before all the others in the fineness of the furnishings and every little luxury that could be teased out of the clutter in the rest of the house. The affection between the brother and sisters was so evident it did not need explanation and Fliss really did envy them that.

Chapter Seven

Delicious. The word Miss Grantham murmured
with such pleasure as she sipped her tea echoed
around in Darius's head as sheer temptation even
now he was riding home at the side of Marianne's
gig. Somehow he had managed to keep Nero to a
pace the hard-worked carriage horse could keep up
with so far, but he needed his attention on his spirited
horse and not tempting young women with delicious
curves he had best learn to forget about.

Miss Grantham looked delicious as well as sounding it when she sat in her hostess's neat sitting room
with the afternoon sun slanting in under the half-
closed blinds, as if it was determined to get in to
highlight the girl in her after months and maybe even
years of sitting in a schoolroom unnoticed by the
wider world. She had dressed in a gown a shade of
light yellow he had never realised until today was the
ideal foil for such fiery locks and clear skin. In wild
contrast to his first impression of her, she looked like

a breath of spring instead of a muddy goddess. It felt as if he had been kicked in the midriff and points south when he furtively eyed her sipping tea. And that gown was cut to make her look so demure and coolly composed that she seemed totally unaware of her own curvaceous appeal in all that fondly clinging muslin and light petticoats. She looked coolly delicious herself, like a lemon ice on a hot day. Good enough to eat in one greedy gulp and go back for more, he decided wryly. And he wanted her, longed to taste, touch and memorise every delicious inch of her clear redhead's skin from top to toe with his tongue and hands and mouth. Which was not doing his plan to forget her and get on with his plan to secure a better life for his sisters any good at all.

'You are very quiet, Darius,' Marianne said with a shrewd sideways look at him riding along at her side as tamely as a farmer escorting a wagon to market.

'Maybe I am tired,' he said mildly.

'Hmm, and maybe Nero will soon learn to fly and get you home even quicker than you left it. Compared to your usual hearty toil that was hardly even half-a-day's work; you only mended a fence, then walked from the house to Brock Wood and back again. We have driven and ridden ten times as far in an afternoon than we did today when we were on campaign and you usually put in a day and a half's work and never admit you are working too hard now. You liked her, though, didn't you?'

'I suppose you mean Miss Grantham?'

'Of course I do. You have not rescued any other damsels in distress today that you forgot to tell me about, I hope?'

'No, and I will agree that she seems to be a polite and unaffected young woman, so why would I *not* like her?'

'I feel decades older than you at times, Brother dear, and do you really think me so stupid you can put me off with such faint praise? Even as another woman I can see what a spectacular figure Miss Grantham has and I am not given to noticing such things under cover of being so stiffly polite and gentlemanly as you were this afternoon that I wonder you did not turn into an effigy on the spot. But if you truly did not notice she is quite out of the common way, I will have to worry about your eyesight from now on as well as everything else.'

He sighed and shook his head to try to tell her it didn't matter, she knew as well as he did that he might look and admire and even like the woman under Miss Grantham's superb figure and eye-catching looks, but he could not afford to do anything about it. His sister seemed unconvinced and she might be right. Given half a chance his cursed body would override his logical mind and he might end up kissing the delicious Miss Grantham if she ever gave him a chance to and that would be a disaster for both of them. He really must find a way to divert his sister from tackling the rest of his life and any marriage prospects he might have head on in her usual ruthless fashion when she wanted to do him good, whether he agreed with her or not. A poor governess was as impossible for him as he was for her. Neither of them had any money and he needed to know a handsome dowry came with any woman he might decide he wanted to marry. Somehow he had to get his land in good order and dower his sisters and Miss Grantham could not help him to do that, so that was an end to the matter. He would just have to ride out Marianne's attempts to undermine his practical scheme to marry for money and not because of a hot, fleeting attraction to a young woman he had never even set eyes on until this morning and should soon be able to forget.

'We should go to the subscription ball Miss Donne was telling you about,' he said rather abruptly. Now it was Marianne's turn to shoot him an exasperated look, then put up a blankly defensive front. What a hopeless pair they were, him and his darling elder sister who had been through so much for love. 'It is high time you had some fun again, Nan. Even little Broadley has been *en fête* for the peace for months now and you know how much you love to dance,' he added, using his old pet name for her to try to get past the blank face she had shown the world since the Bath tabbies looked at her with such shocked disapproval to add to her terrible grief for Daniel Turner and sink her even further into the doldrums. Dan was one of the few truly good men Darius met in the army and why his brother-in-law ever signed up in the first place was beyond him. The price of a commission was all that divided officers from men and it could be a paper-thin barrier at times.

'No, I had all the fun I ever wanted when we danced and sang the nights away in winter quarters, or when Daniel and I could snatch some time together on the march. I loved him far too much to put another man in his place and sooner or later you will have to accept the fact I cannot imagine ever even beginning to love anyone else half as dearly as I loved him. And that would make the man second-best and be so unfair, so I shall never even consider marrying again, Darius. You need to give up on the idea I might change my mind if you push me out of the house often enough to meet the local gentlemen, for they will not thank you for it and neither will I.'

'More fool them,' he said grimly, but he was tempted to let the matter drop. No, he refused to let her wall herself in with duties and made-up tasks here just as she had done in Bath. By the time he got back to England this spring she was so closed in by them and out of sorts with the world around her that he barely recognised his brave, laughing sister in the poor widow who did all the domestic duties in that cramped little house while their mother bemoaned her own hard lot to her friends and did very little of the actual work of running her compact new home. So God bless Great-Uncle Hubert for leaving Owlet Manor to him and giving them both the chance of a new life, but Darius could not let his sister become isolated from her own kind here instead of in Bath. The old house had felt like home the instant they arrived here, but he was not going to let his sister use the excuse of getting his grand and lost-in-time old house tidy and presentable again to wall out the rest of the world.

'I am not asking you to forget him, Marianne, just live as well as you know Daniel would want you to without him. And if that is not reason enough, remember that Viola needs us to establish ourselves in local society so that she will be able to move more easily among them once we have the farms and the house working as they ought to and we can afford to be a family again.'

He actually felt the doubt behind the thoughtful look she shot him as he stared at the road ahead and refused to let his fantasy that both his sisters would one day live at Owlet Manor and enjoy a much better life die. The old place had once provided for a far bigger family than theirs; it must have done for the original family to build such a fine house in the first place, so the land could be that productive again with a lot of hard work and an influx of capital. If he could just improve his stock and introduce some of the new farming methods, the estate would soon begin to thrive again and if he had to marry money to make it happen, so be it. His sisters were not going to sit on the shelf for the rest of their lives because of a lack of resolution on his part and he must find a way to force them off it before it was too late. His

parents had done a poor job of providing for their
daughters and he was determined not to fail them
as well. Since he never intended to fall in love, why
cavil at marrying an heiress for her money?

'I hope Viola will think again about staying in her
current place as well, Darius, and that she will come
to us for a holiday while she thinks about finding
another, but while we were living together in Bath I
realised how much she loves studying and learning
new things, then teaching them to her pupils. She has
no great interest in fashion or the social whirl and
no desire to catch herself a fine husband. Viola en-
joys awakening young minds and helping them track
down answers to all the awkward questions they are
rash enough to ask her. She would have made a fine
don if we lived in a different world.'

'Unlucky for her she was born female, then, and
will be trapped in a lifetime of teaching ladylike accomplishments and household management to girls
who don't much want to learn them if we do not prise
her out of the schoolroom and give her a chance to
raise scholars of her own one day. You know how
little gently bred young women are supposed to know
about the outside world to be thought perfect wife
material. We would have to remake the world for
Viola to be a true scholar.'

'As well I met my Daniel and fell in love with
him, since I hated my books as much as Viola loved
them and I never could seem to fit into Mama's version of a perfect daughter. We would have driven one

another mad, fighting over my potential choices of husband and her version of who he ought to be if I had stayed at home with our parents for much longer after you went off to be a soldier and were not there to back me up any more.'

'I am sorry I deserted you then and that I sent you home to them after Dan died as well, but I promise never to do it again, Nan. As for our little sister, I know as well as you do that Viola is every bit as stubborn as either of us, but if we are ever going to persuade her to live with us and have the sort of life we both know she should have, then there must be some sort of society for her to mix with when she gets here, or she will turn tail and go back to teaching for the rest of her life. You need company as well, even if you refuse to admit it. And I need to meet a lady with a big enough fortune to get Owlet Manor back on its feet, so how am I to do that if you refuse to even join our neighbours' celebrations of the peace with France?'

That was a wrong note; he could tell by the stubborn set of her mouth as she took her turn at staring into the middle distance and looked absolutely determined not to go. Time to replay the sisterly cards he had just fumbled so badly. 'Viola might be swept off her feet by one of the local beaux when she gets here and allow herself to be lured into marriage before she is too old and set in her ways to adapt to a shared life with a fine man.'

'She is only three and twenty. I am the old one.'

'Seven and twenty is not old and don't forget that I am two years ahead of *you*. I badly need to find myself a wealthy young lady prepared to marry me before I become too old and grey for anyone to want me at all.'

'Not if you intend to marry her only for money you don't,' he thought her heard her murmur.

'What else is there?' he said cynically and felt as if he was betraying something newly made and significant by exposing it to the frosty reality that he needed to wed a fortune. He could not betray both of his sisters' best interests by leaping into a love match, whether those sisters realised where their best interests lay or not. Then he recalled the fascinating spectacle of Miss Grantham in all her muddy glory when he had first seen her lit up by midsummer sunlight in the clearing in Brock Wood. He had had to exert all his willpower not to gawp at her like a bemused and instantly randy yokel at the time and an image of her mud-revealed feminine beauty seemed to have burned itself into his mind and senses like a brand, but they had met under unusual circumstances. That accounted for the impact she had made on him.

Normally she would only be one more pleasant-looking young woman among the bevy of unwed females he encountered at any social occasion. If they had seen each other for the first time at this celebration ball to be held at the local posting inn and Assembly Rooms to laud victory over a fallen emperor they would have been civil to one another and parted without a second thought on either side after a polite country dance and a little social conversation. It was only because Miss Grantham was lost in his wood, covered in mud and wet to the skin that she seemed so extraordinary at first sight. Yet when he tried to reason her appeal to his mind and senses away he still could not get a picture of her in her wet and clinging gown and looking like a very dirty wood nymph out of his head.

'There is love,' Marianne said starkly in answer to his foolish question and he had laid himself open to that one, hadn't he? Perhaps for the Daniels and Mariannes of this world, but not for a fool like him and a woman he did not, could not, know any better than he did now.

Chapter Eight

'You are perfectly turned out now, Felicity, and if we do not leave the house soon Mrs Corham will grow impatient and go without us. She knows everyone in Broadley and the surrounding area so we would do well to enter the rooms with her if you are to be accepted as her latest protégée.'

'I am too old to be anyone's protégée.'

'What nonsense and don't forget that I know exactly how old you are. You are still only a girl at four and twenty and it is high time you enjoyed being young before it really is too late.'

Hmm, that sounded like regret for the youth Miss Donne had worn away in schoolrooms up and down the land, so Fliss could not labour the point and bemoan her own late entry into the social whirl, even if it was only little Broadley and the local gentry that would be doing the whirling. 'Are you sure I am neat enough and likely to be able to convince everyone there tonight that I am only a poor governess on holiday?' Fliss asked as she gazed at herself in the shadowy old mirror Miss Donne had placed at the top of the stairs to reflect extra light.

'You have always been far too young and eager for life to be one of those to me, but you really need to learn from Mr Brummell and refuse to tamper with perfection once it has been achieved, so come on, my dear. We will have to be in good time so I can find a good seat in the function room before there is a crush and you know I prefer to sit on the sidelines now that I really am a tabby.'

'You are not a gossipy little lady of uncertain years and I am sorry, I really cannot imagine what has got into me to fuss over my appearance like this. Although I do have a lot more sympathy with poor Juno now I know how nerve-racking it is to make your official debut in society, I promise you I will not give my appearance another thought for the rest of the evening. Imagine how proud you will be when I breezily ignore a rip in my skirts and stains on the bodice as the night goes on.'

'If you ruin any more of your gowns we will have to order more than a humble governess could afford and your little deception will be unmasked.'

'I agree that a vast order of new gowns from the local dressmaker would give me away as far better off than I am pretending to be, so I suppose I had best be careful with this one after all.'

'Yes, and, while I can see why you do not want to be pursued for your money, I really do not see how we can conceal your good fortune for very much longer, Felicity. It will soon become obvious you are making little or no effort to find a new position for yourself. Your last pupil went off to make her debut in polite society over two months ago now and people will soon put two and two together and make half a dozen if we do not tell the truth,' Miss Donne said as if the idea of the very gossip Fliss did not want breaking out had been troubling her for a while.

'I am not sure I could ever learn to like another pupil as much as Juno and please don't ask me to pretend to look for a post. I am not sure I can keep on teaching now I do not have to and I would like a little more time to think about what to do next before news of my inheritance gets out. I doubt an out-and-out fortune hunter would trouble himself with the likes of me if Mrs Frampton was available to outclass me in looks, experience and fortune. She is a far better catch than I am and even if news does get out that I am a lot richer than I seem now, at least she will have had her first pick of the fortune hunters and she does not strike me as a woman to tolerate rivals.'

'Pray do not be vulgar about your money or hers, Felicity. You make it sound like a competition and there is no comparison between the two of you,' Miss Donne said in her best governess manner.

Fliss grimaced and supposed her thoughts must have turned feral since she met Mr Yelverton. Even the thought of him looking dumbstruck by the handsome blonde widow and beguiled by her moneybags made her want to kick something, hard. 'The lady would be the first to agree with me,' she argued lightly, despite a sharp need to scratch the smug Mrs Frampton's face if she ever did catch herself such a fine husband as Mr Yelverton on her well-baited hook.

'Mrs Frampton may have inherited a deal of money from her late husband, but not all the wealth in the Royal Mint could make her into a true lady,' Miss Donne said waspishly.

Fliss shot her friend a thoughtful look before she draped the pretty summer shawl Juno had given her for her last birthday around her shoulders. 'Given her condescending manner when we met in the drapers the other day I would say she thinks otherwise, but what do you know about her that she would prefer you not to?'

'Only that she came from very little despite all her airs and graces and she married a good man for his money, which she has been very busy spending ever since, by the way, so she may not be as rich as you and everyone else thinks she is by now. She will end up back where she began if she is not careful since even her late husband's money will not last for ever at the rate she keeps on spending it.'

'Hmm,' Fliss murmured with a thoughtful look at her friend's averted face. 'I take it the late Mr Frampton was a friend of yours?'

'I knew him quite well as a young man, although I am not sure if we were truly friends. My parents would not have approved if I made a friend of the gardener's boy and I don't suppose his would have either.'

'Mrs Turner obviously did not care what her family thought of her choice of husband,' Fliss said slyly, then felt ashamed when she saw something very like sorrow and regret in her friend's gaze before she turned and led the way downstairs as if they had been talking about the weather.

'Not all of us are brave enough to seize love when it is offered to us, Felicity. Remember that sad fact if it is ever offered to you truly and sincerely and take my advice and grab it with both hands,' Miss Donne said when they were walking through the neat little sitting room and on their way out, as if she had changed her mind about keeping her own secrets close in order to give Fliss the benefit of her own painful experiences.

Fliss hugged her former governess impulsively. 'Thank you, for that sage advice and for caring about me when nobody else did, and for still doing it now I am grown up and should be looking after myself. I have never felt truly lonely since the day we met, although my uncle made me feel I ought to be grateful for every mouthful I ate and every hand-me-down garment of my cousin's I wore while we lived in his house.'

'At least now you are properly grown up I can tell you that I always thought Lord Netherton very foolish to treat his only sister's child so coldly you would have thought her elopement was your fault. Never mind the past now though, my love; I gained and he lost by being so frigid with you. Unlike him you are a warm and loving person and I am honoured to have you as a dear friend now we no longer have to be pupil and teacher to one another, but some of the sorrows of the past really are best forgotten,' her friend said bracingly, then she led the way to the front door before they became maudlin.

'Thank you for everything you have done for me and I love you,' Fliss said because it needed to be spoken instead of danced round as if it was too embarrassing to talk about.

'And I love you, Felicity. You and two other pupils I once taught feel like family to me and you make it so much easier to be a childless spinster so I should be thanking you. Now we really must be on our way or we will be very late and I am looking forward to being at a party where I do not have to pretend I am part of the furniture.'

'I know what you mean,' Fliss said and that was exactly what a governess was supposed to be when she brought her charges downstairs to be petted and exclaimed over and over-excited, before they were sent back to the nurseries to be fractious, overtired and too excited to sleep.

'Then remember the disadvantages of our profession as well as the lovely compensations like you and your own latest pupil when you are deciding what to do next, my dear, but now let us hurry and neither

of us need worry about disapproving employers tonight so let us enjoy our freedom and worry about
tomorrow when it comes.'

'Very well,' Fliss said and she felt her heart lift at
the idea of a whole evening of not being a respectable governess to look forward to.

Miss Donne rarely spoke of her feelings, but she
had just admitted Fliss was far more important than
just a former pupil to her. She had been kind, unsen-
timental and steady as rock whenever Fliss needed
advice or support over the years and she wished she
was only half as good at being guide and mentor to
Juno. That reminded her, she must write to her former pupil again and try to be as wise and steady for
Juno as her own governess had always been for her.
She followed Miss Donne across the neat little square
to Mrs Corham's house opposite, still wondering if
it could ever be right to risk everything for such an
elusive and insubstantial emotion as romantic love.
Her parents had taken that risk and left her all alone
and grieving for them because they could not endure
being parted even for her sake. Marianne had em-
braced it and ended up bereft and grieving as well.

Yet Fliss still wondered how it might feel to dance
with a gentleman as handsome, dashing and powerful as Mr Yelverton tonight instead of sitting in some
lonely alcove waiting for her pupils to be ready for a
quick exit and bed. She had been trying to convince
herself he was not particularly special ever since they
waved him and his sister goodbye after he rescued

her the other day. Now a spark of delicious anticipation was making her heartbeat skip and butterflies dance in her belly at the very thought of taking to the dance floor with him so she had not succeeded very well, had she?

So how was a gentleman supposed to react to extreme temptation when he was wearing tight evening breeches and a cutaway coat? Badly, Darius decided and thanked heaven for the crowd of revellers determined to enjoy themselves after long years of fear and war and the heavy taxation to pay for it all. He ducked behind a knot of red-faced and perspiring gentlemen who were probably too old to have danced quite so vigorously or toasted the peace as enthusiastically and cursed the day he first set eyes on Miss Grantham in her all-but-naked glory. He ached for the inconvenient female. He risked another glance at her dancing with some lecher who was not quite the gallant idiot she clearly thought. Not that he could blame the man for sweating and looking as if he could hardly believe his luck as he jigged about far too vigorously so that his dance partner had to as well. Obviously the fool was delighted to be in heady feminine company and Darius's fists itched to wipe the jackal smile off his face. Miss Grantham looked delightful in a plain muslin gown the colour of rich cream and all the more alluring because she did not seem to have the slightest idea how utterly desirable she was.

He could hear a tabby tut-tutting nearby at the spectacle of a mere governess fascinating so many men without even appearing to try. But even that sour old biddy could not find anything to complain about in Miss Grantham's modest gown with its demure bodice and plain skirts as befitted a lady previously engaged to teach dancing and other ladylike accomplishments to her pupils, rather than expect to dance in it herself. The gown was still made of soft and creamy muslin, though, the sort of filmy, almost-not-there type of cloth he recognised from his little sister's best gowns. Even if they were worn over however many light petticoats it took to make them opaque to searching male gazes, the soft, light stuff was so finely woven and delicately made up it must be ideal for wearing on such a warm night but, oh, how it clung to Miss Grantham's glorious body whenever she moved in the figures of the dance. A more elaborate gown with fashionable belled-out skirts and more fuss and frills than Darius wanted to think about would not have had anything like as much charm for him and all the other gentlemen noticing how wonderfully simplicity became a lady tonight. Her gown whispered around her neatly slender legs and outlined her sweetly curved hips when she moved up and down the line in the weave through the other couples in the dance. And when she twisted and turned in time to the music the drape of it around her tiny waist and not-at-all tiny bosom made him groan out loud and be very glad the music was so loud. He was a satyr. He was not here to leer at a governess who had no idea how utterly delightful she looked as she moved in time to the music. The reason he came here tonight was purely mercenary, if you discounted his concern that Marianne was in danger of cutting herself off from the rest of the world at Owlet Manor. He had come here to meet a rich woman and hope he could charm her into marrying him so she could be lady of the manor and he could repair his roof in time for the winter and buy a ram and all the other things the farms needed to drag them into the nineteenth century.

So there was the antidote to this heat and heady desire for a woman he could never have if he was to achieve any of that. He would dance with Mrs Frampton and fawn on Miss Pelham, who was rumoured to have twenty thousand pounds in her dower chest, and he could excuse a squint and the odd crooked tooth in a woman with such a handsome dowry. Except he had his doubts about Miss Pelham; she might be plain and overeager to be married for her money, but she deserved better in a husband. Mrs Frampton it would have to be, then. He felt nothing at all for her, not even much admiration for hair he was worldly wise enough to know was dyed blonde and a body he suspected had been padded out and pulled in where she thought it should be to give the impression there was more to her than there really was. The woman was as artificial as a paper flower. He gulped down a glass of brandy for Dutch courage and steeled himself to ask the merry widow for the supper dance.

'Oh, here you are at last, Darius,' Marianne observed as he tried to ghost past her at the edge of the ballroom without being noticed. She clamped a firm grasp on his upper arm as if she had read his mind and intended to sabotage his plan. 'Miss Grantham will be quite worn out after such a vigorous dance and in dire need of a quiet corner to recover from her exertions and a wolf to scare that fat puppy away. As you are the only one we have handy, you will just have to do.'

'How much punch have you drunk tonight?' he murmured as the frenetic note in her voice worried him.

'Both too much and not enough,' she muttered back as if she really meant it. He began to wonder if making her come out tonight against her wishes had been such a good idea and she certainly did not look as if she intended to meekly sit by and watch him courting heiresses tonight.

'I am sure I can summon up a stern enough glare to make that overeager young man go away and find someone else's toes to tread on, Marianne,' Miss Donne intervened before he could argue with his sister's bleak summary of her evening. 'But if you could procure us some lemonade I would be most grateful, Mr Yelverton, and I am sure Miss Grantham will be even more so after so much exertion.'

'Of course, ma'am, I would be delighted,' he lied and did his best to look it even so.

Miss Donne eyed the noisy knot of gentlemen looking red-faced and rather glassy eyed and shook her head. 'I cannot help thinking the wilder elements present must have thought it a fine joke to add a bottle or two of Wellow's best apple brandy to the fruit cup, so it might be as well to avoid it,' she said.

'Lemonade it is then,' he agreed meekly and tried to feel disappointed about missing the perfect chance to dance with Mrs Frampton.

Fate played a mean trick on him on his way back, laden with drinks from the refreshment room, when Mrs Frampton took the initiative he had been trying to create all evening and slipped into his path like a very well-corseted snake.

'Ooh, lemonade, how cooling and delightful. So very thoughtful of you, Mr Yelverton,' she gushed and snatched a glass from the plate he had improvised with instead of a tray. She gulped it down as theatrically as if he had brought her sherbet from the nearest sultan's harem at the end of a long quest for her favours.

'Glad to be of service, madam,' he murmured shortly and stepped stiffly away from her reaching hands, refusing a golden opportunity to fascinate a wealthy and very willing widow and maybe even get them both thoroughly compromised in this unexpected gloom.

'Surely you are not going to leave me here alone

and in the dark, Mr Yelverton?' she added throatily and sounded so silkily certain she could make him forget the ladies he had set out to find these drinks for that his hackles rose.

'It was quite light in here when I passed through only a few moments ago,' he said with a wary glance at all the guttered candles and failed lamps nearby. 'Good evening to you, Mrs Frampton,' he said with a stiff bow, then he walked away from fifty-thousand hard-earned Frampton pounds without a backward glance.

Maybe Broadley was not a big enough town to hold an heiress with looks and personality, a sense of humour and a fine figure to keep him intrigued, faithful and fascinated for the rest of his life. A mythical golden dolly who looked and acted exactly like Miss Grantham would do him very nicely, but that really was a fantasy.

'Only three glasses, Brother dear?' Marianne twitted him when he arrived back at the corner of the function room Miss Donne had appropriated for her party.

'The fourth met with an accident so I left it behind,' he said, concentrating all his efforts on resisting the urge to tug Miss Grantham out of her seat and lead her into that conveniently dark corner he had quit so hastily, so he could kiss her in peace and compromise them as soon as someone followed in his footsteps on their way from the refreshment room.

'Best find a waiter and get him to fetch another

and the glass of whatever you were going to drink as well,' his sister said blandly.

'Thank you for that totally unnecessary piece of advice, little Sister,' he said repressively.

'All very well, I can wait for a cool drink,' she went on, 'but Miss Grantham has been dancing until her poor feet must be begging for mercy.'

Darius sighed and silently admitted it was a mistake to make his sister come here on such a frantically merry night and get frantically merry to keep the memories at bay. Even so she must be reminded of nights of wild dancing and improvised music in Portugal and Spain, when Marianne still had Daniel to be wild and merry with. They would rejoice at being alive, swap funny stories and dance until they were all nearly ready to drop. Then Daniel would take her home to wherever they had made one for the week, or even the night, and presumably keep her awake a little longer. He felt the same rush of guilt and pity that used to nearly overwhelm him every time he got back to his tent or billet for the night after Daniel died to find his strong and determined sister rocking herself back and forth on the ground, almost consumed by grief.

'Thank you very much, Mr Yelverton. A cooling drink really is most welcome after such an energetic dance,' Miss Grantham interrupted his sombre thoughts with a quizzical look and a wry smile to silently agree, yes, her new friend was a little bit merry, but now they knew what was causing it her

friends would drown all that apple brandy in lemonade and save her a dreadful headache in the morning.

'My pleasure, ma'am,' he said sombrely.

He hoped she had no idea he was wondering if
she would taste of lemon if he kissed her. The other
day she looked so kissable in yellow muslin he was
imagining her in lemon-coloured silk instead. He
tortured himself with fantasies of taking her home
tonight to see how she tasted under the whisper of
fine silk. The pleasure might be all his if he was
not careful, but it was only a fantasy. It could never
happen. He had to keep reminding himself how impossible she was all the way back to the inn where
they had left the gig, then onwards to his lonely bed
at Owlet Manor.

Ma'am? she mouthed as if she was surprised he
could treat her so stiffly after their long and memorable walk back from Brock Wood the other day.

He meant to nod emphatically and let her know
that was how things were going to be between them
from now on, but the mischief in her dark eyes defeated him as she shook her head and shot him a
witchy, challenging look.

'There, I have nearly got my breath back and
I think my toes have almost recovered,' she said
blandly, but why would she risk dancing with a rogue
like him after her experiences with the last one? If
that was what she was hinting she wanted to do, of
course, and he was not imagining she did because
he did, too.

'Have you forgotten how to dance since you left the army, Darius?' his sister asked and even Miss Donne was smiling encouragingly, as if he was a callow youth who might be too shy to ask a lady to dance without a little benign encouragement. If only they knew how little encouragement he needed where Miss Felicity Grantham was concerned, they might not be so eager to push him at her as a dance partner, he decided gloomily.

'No, Sister dear, I have not. Will you honour me with the next dance, Miss Grantham?' he forced himself to say politely as the local band tuned up.

'I wanted to dance just one dance with a gentleman I know will not tread on my toes or leer at me every time we meet up in the dance,' she confided softly as they were making their way towards the couples already on the dance floor.

'Has it been such an ordeal?' he asked. If only she knew how badly he wanted to kiss her she would not have such touching confidence in his gentlemanly instincts.

'It has been an unusual sort of evening so far, but at least I can admit to the bruises I had before it began with you. I now have a few more to add to the score and remind me what a clumsy fool I was the other day.'

'Not at all,' he said stiffly and wondered what she would say if he forgot the moves of the dance and stumbled over her feet for the sheer bewilderment of being this close to her again. 'They are the clumsy idiots for treading on your toes.'

'Maybe they were bedazzled by my extraordinary beauty,' she said with an endearing chuckle as she shook her head at him to say she was joking. 'Or perhaps it is lack of practice and too much rum punch,' she added as they finally joined the other couples.

He could not tell her she was right the first time. She was quite lovely and blinded him to any other pretty girls here tonight. 'You should make allowances for your effect on us dumb males, Miss Grantham,' he murmured as he took her gloved hand for the opening measure and felt a charge of something he did not want to think about flash between them like hot lightning.

'Oh, don't you start as well,' she murmured back as they moved forward with nods and social smiles for the others in this measure. Just as well nobody could tell he was so conscious of her every move he had no idea who they were. Miss Felicity Grantham was holding his hand so the rest of the crowd in this stuffy room might as well be invisible now. Ah, now she was standing away from him and waiting for the next couple to make their moves. So he could hardly blame her for this fierce focus on her vivid hair and delightful figure when he could not even see her over the top of the idiots gigging about in his way. He had to concentrate fiercely on the moves of the dance as he fought the temptation to elbow his way through and make sure she was not being ogled by any more leering boors while his back was turned.

'Ah, there you are,' he said inanely when they were allowed to stand together again and she looked unharmed and definitely not flustered, so the gentlemen must have behaved this time.

'Yes, here I am,' she teased him, but he was not in a teaseable mood tonight—he might end up dangerous if she was not more careful.

And so it went on, her darting through the movements of the dance so nimbly he wished she was larger and more immobile so he could keep a better eye on her, him going through the motions and longing to stand over her like a grumpy bear, so no other man would dare to use his height to get a better view of her delightful bosom from above. He had been quite right to try to avoid this until it would have been rude not to ask her for a dance. And he had never had to try to dance at the same time as he was fighting an urge to punch any adult male who might watch his dance partner with lusty eyes until tonight. He wanted it to be only them in the room. Perhaps the town band could play on in the next room, so they could dance alone and the men in it could not leer at her either. Yet how could he feel possessive and protective of a woman he hardly knew? He had been quite right to greet her briskly, then make an excuse about being needed on the farm the other day when she came to Owlet Manor with Miss Donne to thank Marianne again for her kindness. Then what must the confounded woman do but offer to help with the mountain of sewing they found his sister struggling with? Now he had to stay out on the farms all day while she proved herself to be a proper friend and came back day after day to help Marianne with this or that task she could make a little less strenuous and more fun with her help and company. He could not begrudge his sister a good friend, even if he caught himself sniffing for a trace of the rosewater and Fliss scent of her in the little parlour when he entered it at twilight, after he could be certain she was gone.

'Thank goodness that's over,' he mumbled disagreeably when the players hit a fine crescendo, then wound to rather a ragged halt.

'Indeed,' she said haughtily, then bowed to their fellow dancers before leading the way back to her friend as if she could not imagine where he had come from.

'That must have gone well,' Marianne murmured in his ear as he waited for Miss Grantham to be seated, then took the seat beside his sister.

'Less of your sarcasm, madam, and kindly stop interfering,' he muttered back dourly, but she just raised her eyebrows at him and sought her new friend Mrs Corham's advice on the best way to clean antique lace without ruining it. She seemed to have sobered up while he was busy being bad tempered on the dance floor and at least that was a good thing.

'The waiter brought more lemonade while you were dancing, my dear, and whatever that is for you,

Mr Yelverton,' Miss Donne told him kindly, as if he needed some consolation for what must have been a disastrous dance with her protégée, since they were avoiding looking at one another so carefully. 'It is getting very hot in here and those gentlemen are very far from sober,' she added with a disapproving frown at a corner of the room where some of the guests were swapping warm stories and laughing uproariously.

'You two young things need a few moments to get your breath back and recover after your exertions on the dance floor, but then I believe we should leave,' Mrs Corham said with a hard stare at the rowdy group turning this celebration of peace into a near riot. 'We can enjoy a quiet interlude in my rose garden before you have to go home and it will certainly be a lot more peaceful there.'

'Thank you, ma'am, I would love to,' Miss Grantham said before Darius could say no, it was time they left for Owlet Manor. 'Do say you will come, Marianne. It is too early to sleep and too late for you to sit down with all that mending when you get home. We still have time to celebrate the Allied Victory a little more quietly before you have to go back to Owlet Manor.'

'Yes, my dear; do forget all the tasks that await you there for this one night at least,' Miss Donne encouraged his sister with a kind smile. How could he argue when they were right, Marianne would find something to do if they went home now and she would probably pretend she was not sad and wistful while she was doing it.

Darius eyed the drunken fools who thoughtlessly turned a celebration of peace rowdy with contempt and wondered if he was getting old. The stupid young idiots were trying to throw one of their number from the steps that led up to the rooms when wiser heads intervened. As those wiser heads exchanged resigned glances and bore their offspring off to dunk them in the nearest horse trough the ball was obviously going to break up early anyway. Whoever adulterated this punch had caused a merry night to descend into drunken farce and they ought to be ashamed. Even some of the ladies were giggling tipsily and seemed flushed with far more than the heat of the dance but at least Marianne seemed a lot more sober now.

What an idiot he was to think his darling sister could put aside her grief for Daniel and dance the night away with other men. Now he would have to endure Miss Grantham's incendiary presence all the way to Mrs Corham's and for a while after they got there, but he could not deny Marianne a peaceful interlude with her new friends before they drove home in the moonlight after a difficult evening.

Chapter Nine

'Thank you, Miss Grantham,' Darius muttered in her ear as they strolled through the market square and into the better streets of the town. At least out here the moon cast long shadows and he could get close enough to whisper so Marianne could not hear and realise she was the reason why he had to say it.

'What for?'

'For realising how hard Marianne was struggling to cope with all that gaiety. Most of the people there tonight have no idea what sacrifices had to be made so they could have this peace they are so wild about.'

'Your sister suffered a grievous loss,' she told him rather stiffly.

'I know it,' he said just as stiffly back.

'And I admire her courage and loyalty,' she added doggedly.

'As do I.'

'Miss Donne will be a good friend to her after I

leave Broadley,' she added as if her departure was imminent.

And why was his heart racing with panic at the idea he might not see her again for many years? 'Do you have a new position to go to, then?' he asked.

'Not as yet; but I have had an offer. I am not quite sure it is the right situation for me or whether I am the correct fit for the person who made it,' she said as if the very idea of it made her feel uneasy.

He felt fiercely protective and wished she did not need to work at all. If only Great-Uncle Hubert's wondrous legacy had come with a nice neat fortune he could court a poor governess and forget his scruples about marrying a wife he could so easily learn to love. 'Going to work for a new family must be a challenge,' he said and frowned. How would his sister Viola feel when *her* pupils no longer needed their governess? Although she could have another decade of service ahead or her, given the spread of ages her current pupils covered, and he didn't like that idea very much either.

'Indeed,' Miss Grantham said as if measuring her words.

'I suppose the wider family of the girl you have just finished teaching might offer you a post,' he said encouragingly. Try as he might to pretend that was a good idea, the still-luminous sky even this late in the day at this time of year and the fact of her walking next to him kept tugging at his senses and whispering of a better life for her if she married him and they worked hard for all the things he was trying to take a shortcut to by fortune hunting. He could not offer Miss Grantham a future of insecurity and hardship at his side and this physical wanting would fade; it was too sudden and rampant to have deep roots in their everyday lives. Yet the scent of rosewater and woman so close that he only had to reach for her argued otherwise.

'Sometimes a position does come from a personal recommendation,' she said distantly, as if he had crassly reminded her she was only here on holiday.

'Better the devil you know,' he persisted lamely, but why was he so eager to find out where she was going next? It was not as if he was planning to visit her.

'Perhaps,' she said as if preoccupied with thoughts of a life he could not even begin to imagine.

Well, she was wrong, he could. Not that he particularly liked the picture of isolation and careless snubs his imagination was feeding him. 'It must be hard to go to a new place where you have no idea of the true temper or inclinations of the family who have engaged you.'

'Yes, that can be very difficult at first,' she said stiffly.

Miss Donne's friend Mrs Corham had turned round to wait for them at a finely wrought gate and what must be her fine house beyond it. Dangerous for him to be so absorbed in Miss Grantham he totally forgot his sister and their chaperons were walking a little way ahead. The whole world would realise Miss Grantham fascinated Mr Yelverton if he was not careful and he could not afford to marry her.

'Welcome,' Mrs Corham said with an expansive gesture at the elegant modern house on the very edge of the town that hugged the hillside like a lover and must offer a fine view of the surrounding country-side by daylight. 'I know you do not have enough room for people in your garden now it is planted so thickly with your beloved flowers, Eleanor Donne,' she told her friend with mock severity. 'We would be sure to fall into some precious rose bush or kick over a beloved pot of never-to-be-replaced curiosities if we risked resorting to *your* garden as a peaceful place to end such a noisy and overheated evening,' the lady said with a smile in her voice.

Darius guessed she was curious about what he and Miss Grantham had been saying to one another in the shadows, but her manners were far too good for her to drop coy hints and make her guests feel self-conscious.

'Miss Donne has developed a fierce passion for horticulture now she has a garden of her own,' Miss Grantham agreed as if she welcomed such an every-day subject after their stiff words and his awkward-ness on the way here.

And she was right. If he gave in to his instincts and courted a refined, educated and virtually penni-less lady like her and she agreed to love, honour and obey him now and again for the rest of their days, they would soon end up in the basket. Marianne and Daniel would have denied it with their last breath, but they taught him a valuable lesson. They were happy as larks on their nothing much a year, but his sister had been totally bereft and left more or less penniless when Daniel died. Marianne's desperate grief for Daniel and her plight trapped in their parents' house, knowing they were secretly relieved to be done with such a son-in-law, told him to avoid incendiary females like Miss Felicity Grantham from now on, for her sake as well as his own.

'For all you pretend to be indifferent to the horticultural arts, Lucy Corham, you have had a very fine garden planted here,' Miss Donne replied to her friend's criticism with a half-serious defence of her new obsession.

'True,' their hostess said rather smugly.

Many of the trees that must shade the gardens pleasantly by daylight now supported strings of nightlights in small glass jars and bowls and made wandering around it in the half-dark seem even more inviting. Dangerous, Darius decided, heading for the group of chairs their hostess must have had set out on the lawn with such an end to the evening in mind. Seeing the ladies seated was a gentleman's duty and Darius was the only one asked to this impromptu garden party. He suspected both older ladies were determined matchmakers at heart and could not even excuse his own sister from doing it as well and she should know better. Marianne sat back in her chair with a theatrical sigh of relief, as if she was decades older than her years. She looked fixed there for the night and Darius shot her an accusing look that she regally ignored.

'Tea, I think, Putkin, and is there any lemonade left?' Mrs Corham asked the manservant who had appeared at her side as if by magic.

'Cook made some more while you were away, madam,' the ghost-like retainer said gloomily and departed for the kitchens.

'He will take for ever to bring it out. Perhaps you two young things would like to take a stroll around the rose garden while we old ladies gossip about the party and rest our weary bones,' Mrs Corham more or less ordered Darius and Miss Grantham.

So he had been right to worry—Mrs Corham was part of this foolish conspiracy and Marianne was sitting firmly in her chair so she must be compliant with the idea, if not actively encouraging this folly. 'Miss Grantham?' he said, offering her his arm with what he hoped was a resigned look that would disguise the leap of eagerness his heartbeat tattooed at the very idea of being stupidly intimate with her in the shadowy garden beyond that first row of lights.

'Mr Yelverton?' she replied coolly, laying the tips of her fingers on his sleeve as they moved stiffly away from the safety of a group and under the candlelit archway into the rose garden beyond, where their lax chaperons would claim they could just about see them, if they strained their eyes against the night and the neatly clipped yew hedges.

'Managing females,' he murmured disgustedly and surprised an endearing little snort of laughter out of her, even if it was muffled behind her hand. It made him want to stifle it even more effectively, but he could not kiss her; that would take them into another country altogether.

'We need not stay out here for long, Mr Yelverton. A quick sniff at one or two of the nearest roses, a brief admiration for Mrs Corham's arbour and that little statue of Flora I can see at the heart of it, and we will be able to go back and take tea together like a pair of dowagers,' she murmured.

His turn to grin at the image of them gossiping over the teacups, heads so close he could reach out and curl one of her fiery ringlets around his forefinger and examine the feel, softness and weight of it properly, or should that be improperly? It should be hot to the touch, he decided, and added that to the picture in his head, surprised when he rubbed his forefinger absently against his thumb to find there was nothing there. There should be a smooth-as-satin and hot-as-pure-sin red curl he could wind around his manly digit like a silky fire, drawing her gently closer and closer with the soft fact of it until she was only a breath away. They would be lip to lip, mouth to mouth as every bit of her reached out to every bit of him, as if they were born to be that close, so truly intimate with one another it was fate and no point in fighting it. No! Where the devil had that wild fantasy of them as lovers come from? She was a lady, for goodness sake. He was a very encumbered gentleman who owed his duty to a woman with a fortune in her dower chest and open to the idea of marriage with a convenient gentleman and his ancient manor house.

'Flora, you say?' he asked clumsily.

'Yes, the Roman goddess of flowers and wheat,' she said, like a long-suffering governess explaining facts to a slow pupil.

Despite having to grit his teeth because he wanted to kiss her until she knew he was a mature and potent male, he managed to keep his hands off her somehow. He never knew the scent of roses could threaten to intoxicate a man as potently as good wine. Add the spice and challenge of her to the already heady mix of candlelight and moonlight and it was enough to drive a man insane with need to see his lover stripped bare and eager under his exploring hands and mouth. He should never have had that reckless second glass of punch, as if daring the devil to do his worst.

'Oh, yes, her,' he said lamely and felt her wary dark eyes focus on him as if she was not quite sure about his sobriety either. He wanted to stare into them and finally find out what colour they were more than ever before, as if he could in the dark. '*That* Flora.' He grasped the topic like a drowning man clinging to a buoy.

'I was not aware of any others.'

How could she sound so coolly amused? She

would not if she could read his mind, though he was delighted she could not. She was such an innocent under that quaint governess-in-charge authority of hers and she had no idea how inflammatory her air of sceptical wisdom was to the rampant male he was tonight. What the devil had those oafs put in the punch? He had drunk rough wine on the march and still marched on the next day, so he ought to have a far harder head than this. Something had rocked him off course and he could not let it be Miss Grantham's proximity in the moonlight; he would not allow it to be that, so it must be adulterated punch.

Fliss wanted to be in two places at once. Caution said back at Miss Donne's in her neat little bed, but eagerness and curiosity said at Owlet Manor in the sure-to-be dilapidated main bedchamber, with the master of the house very awake and aware of her there with him and both of them as naked as the day they were born. And rampantly magnificent she was sure he would be as well. She was a bit foggy about the details of human sexual congress, but suspected they might be a bit like the rest of nature. Not as harsh and solely driven by the instinct to mate as the deer in Stratford Park had been in the autumn, she hoped; it certainly did not seem very likely if this hot thrill of excitement deep inside her was any indication of human mating habits. At the very thought of doing such a thing with this particular man she felt her inner woman threaten to melt and her nipples ache for something she knew she should not want to understand any better, or long to find out what came next. Since she had never felt it before, how could she know if this was the other half of wanting a man as a mature and sensual woman might want one in her lonely bed tonight, or just too much wine and moonlight at the end of an evening when this very man had only reluctantly asked her to dance with him?

But he was endearingly awkward all of a sudden and she could not bring herself to tell him he was an idiot and march away. She really hoped he had no idea how she was feeling, though, but what if she was an open book to him and he didn't want to open it any further? That would be the ultimate humiliation, so maybe she ought to go away just in case. If he could read her foggy thoughts of all the deeply intimate things they could do together in the privacy of his bedchamber, she was sunk. If he knew how much she wanted him to kiss her and he was revolted by the very idea, she would feel as if the bottom had dropped out of her world. So she stiffened and backed away from him as if he had slapped her.

'Careful,' he warned sharply and grabbed her arm to stop her toppling over the edge of the little ornamental pond at the foot of Flora's fountain.

It must stem from a spring and the natural slope of the land made the lazy little fountain possible, she supposed numbly as she watched moon and candlelight sparkle off the gentle rush of cool water. It tumbled into the stone basin she had just been on the verge of falling into.

'You really ought to fight this habit of falling over whenever you are near water, Miss Grantham,' he said with a smile in his deep voice she ought not to be so eagerly on the listen for. He still sounded far too composed and her breathing had speeded up although he was just being a polite gentleman and his touch was almost impersonal.

'I should?' she said huskily and now they were much too close. And out of sight of their supposed chaperons at the heart of Mrs Corham's surprisingly romantic version of a formal rose garden as well.

'Yes; danger can lurk in the most unlikely places,' he added huskily and he should know; he was the biggest one of all.

He must have felt the fine tremor that shook her because he was so close and his hold on her had softened and changed. He gave a great sigh—as if this was something he had been fighting all night and now it was going to happen anyway. He gently tugged her away from her precarious stance on the edge of the sunken stone bowl where the stream had been channelled to splash gently at Flora's bare feet and he was right about the water, her feet were only splashed with cool spring water this time and it felt blissful in the still warmth of the night, so at least one part of her was cool while the rest was heating up like a furnace. She could not claim to be standing on rocky ground now there was closely mown grass

under her feet again, but it felt unsteady under her
feet because he was a mere breath away. She stepped
a little closer even as he pulled her even further in,
conspired with her deepest, darkest womanly urges
to take that last inch of space away from between
them. She felt her breath come short and fast and
parted her lips to gasp a little more air in. When she
slicked her suddenly dry lips with her tongue he gave
a faint groan and bent forward an extra fraction of
an inch so his mouth was gentle on hers for a waiting moment.

It felt as if they had been made for one another, as
if they fitted like two halves of a whole. They hesitated between gentle and pure need and she gave a
small snuffle of a plea she might be embarrassed
about later, then snuggled even closer to his mighty
body without making any of the maidenly protests
she ought to if she was a truly virtuous woman. He
shifted his stance so they could fit closer together and
little flashes of lightning seemed to spark inside her
everywhere they touched all over her; all over him
fire was ready to break out and his mouth slanted and
she opened hers hungrily. Intimacy she had never
even let herself dream of until now flared to life between them and it felt utterly glorious. She had good
instincts, she decided foggily as their mouths clung
hotly and played like lovers'. No, they *were* lovers.
Never mind the details; never mind the denial she
felt somewhere in him beyond all this heat and light
and did not want to think about. Right now, they

were lovers. The everyday Fliss had melted away and a new one stood in her place and she was brazen.

She murmured something encouraging and bent into his embrace like a wanton, standing on tiptoe to delightedly stretch her torso against the solidly muscled wall of his chest, so temptingly waiting to be explored when she was not quite so busy with his mouth. It all felt so intriguing and right she never wanted him to stop kissing her, never wanted his hands to halt an urgent exploration of her supple back and down over the womanly flare of her hips. He ran his tongue along the lush line of her lips where he had kissed them to swollen eagerness and she sighed and added another novelty to her list. He was licking at her plush, kiss-stung mouth now and she opened it and his tongue was in her mouth before she even knew how much she had longed for that intimacy, but only with him.

She felt sensually explored, gloriously open and closer to another being than she had ever thought it was possible to be until now. Experimentally she copied him, a little hesitantly at first, but then she tangled her tongue with his and felt her inner woman jump another level of joyous anticipation. That Fliss was dancing to a rhythm she had only ever been able to guess at before tonight. So *this* was wanting; *this* was mutual fire and heady anticipation of some ultimate delight she did not even dare think about just yet. She moaned very low and not sounding at all like herself as the driving want inside her began to catch up with the beat of their dance—mouth on mouth, tongue on tongue. It was the sweetest beat she had ever felt and it was shattering her willpower into fragments one note at a time. And it might be sweet and heady and wonderful, but it was demanding as well—aching, she amended as she felt the drive and need of it fiery and urgent in her feminine core.

He lowered his hands from cupping her head and caressed her suddenly so-sensitive neck with his deliciously exploring touch, then made even more mischief through the respectable muslin of her gown. Her breast ached for his caresses, as if they knew more than she did about man and woman together in the ultimate intimacy. She felt him adore her already lush breasts with wondering hands, as if they were not even an inch too generous for him and her nipples tightened hard as pebbles in lusty anticipation of more. Nothing had prepared her for the rightness of his long, strong, slightly rasped-with-work fingers delicately teasing her tightly hot nipples like a connoisseur of feminine urgency. His hum of masculine approval as they peaked even more under his touch shot fire to the heated centre of her being and she wanted to moan a husky demand for more, but the little bit of native caution left to her argued no, that would definitely give away what they were doing to one another in the shadows of Mrs Corham's rose garden.

A beat she sensed was old as time and Adam and Eve and new as yesterday had her longing to know even more about lovemaking than he had already taught her. Ah, how desperately she wanted to moan with need and thrust her now-aching breasts fully into his magical hands, wanted him to get them both naked and into a bedchamber at this very moment. What came next must be infinitely private and only for them. But a whisper of discretion; a last little voice shouting this was wrong and impossible right here and right now stopped her keening for more. Respectable people were close by. They thought she was a sensible and mature governess on holiday, a woman who could be trusted to behave herself in a candlelit grove with a handsome man, while they drank tea and talked about their eventful evening only yards away. She still wriggled a little closer to Captain Darius and mentally stuck out her tongue at her inner governess. This chance to feel everything, to know true passion, might never come again so she was not going to let it pass her by. She hid a little smile against his mouth as he kissed her again, as if it was the only way he could keep himself from groaning out his need for everything they could give one another as lovers, too.

They were obviously very bad people and she loved it. His stroking hands were fully on the cheeks of her bottom now as his mouth drove her further into heat than she had ever been before. He was cupping her so he could pull her close in to his very potent male member and that was obviously fully aroused, she confirmed to him with another of those secret, gloating smiles. If he had not been himself and uniquely desirable she would have been revolted and shot away from him like a startled doe. As it was him the rampant, unarguable truth of it made her feel even hotter and more desperate for him and a little bit flattered as well. All those Greek statues Uncle Netherton thought he had safely hidden away in his so-called Temple of Virtues had done nothing to prepare her for how large and driven and rigid a man's sex went when he so obviously needed a woman. Darius very definitely wanted her right here and right now. She ignored the last whisper of caution and galloped on towards whatever would come next in the velvety shadows he had pulled her into when this became a lot more serious than a careless kiss in the shadows.

Then, over at the opposite side of this paradise garden, where the real world still lived, someone dropped what sounded like a teaspoon on to the stone terrace. It was as faint as an echo in the stillness of the warm summer night and loud as the crack of doom and it woke her up from her sensuous dream of impossible things. She jumped backwards so violently she was nearly on the edge of that fountain bowl before she remembered about Flora's gentle waterfall and managed to stop herself before she fell right in. Had they really been so reckless, so unwary of the night?

Yes, they most definitely had, she decided and stood watching him, her mouth open wide in shock at what they had almost done and desperate to know what he thought about it. She gazed up at him and despaired of ever finding her usual cool logic again in the hazy mess he had made of her thoughts with those earth-shattering, life-changing kisses. He had undone her in every way but the obvious one. Somehow her laces were still neatly in place, the neck of her gown was as demure as ever over her hot and needy breasts. Even her hair had not quite managed to tumble out of its pins, despite his caressing touch, and betray her as far too susceptible to Mr Darius Yelverton's sensuous, careless attentions.

And they were careless, she could see that now. He had already stepped back and away from her and was looking coolly distant as a snow-covered mountain, despite the mighty evidence of his rigid desire for her she had gloried in so naively only seconds ago. Surely he could not deny the fact of it even as he distanced himself from her? Apparently he could; any minute now he might turn into a statue of the perfect soldier in his best civilian garb as he froze that evidence into submission and pretended it had never been so explicit between them that she could never have made him up. It was all a mistake, then; a wild urge to explore something she ought not to even want to explore with another man when she was so very nearly engaged to her former employer's son. The thought of Lord Stratford and that very proper and logical marriage proposal he had made her before he left for France was a sobering one. It felt as if she had stepped back into Flora's marble fountain bowl of cool, clear spring water and startled her true self back to life when this man stared at her with chilly horror, as if he had been misled by moonlight and rashly raised ridiculous hopes in her spinsterly breast.

Lord Stratford thought she would make an ideal wife for a diplomat, but he did not know about this part of her, did he? Even she had not known about this Fliss, not until she set eyes on the stranger who rescued her from his woods not even a week ago. But Darius Yelverton no more wanted to want her than she wanted to want him, if this was what happened when you returned to earth after such a heady flight into enchantment and all that loss of self in a man's arms. So all they had ever had was mutual attraction and mutual reluctance—what a terrible tie that would have been to bind themselves together with for life if they had been left out here undisturbed for just a few fragile moments longer.

'I am sorry,' he said stiffly and confirmed her worst fears.

'So am I,' she replied sharply and she was. She was sorry for her inner sensualist because that wild version of her was never going to find fulfilment. Even sorrier for Miss Grantham who dared to hope there was more to life than teaching other people's children or a sensible marriage with a sensible man. Better settle for a marriage of convenience than give in to animal passions like those Mr Yelverton had aroused in her tonight then pay for the consequences of that folly for the rest of their lives. That was all it had been for him then, just lust. Now he was eyeing her as if he hardly knew which way she was going to jump next and he fervently hoped it was in the opposite direction from him. How could she even think about more of his drugging, delightful kisses when he did not want to be enchanted by them? So neither did she; they were lies of the worst sort.

'We must go back,' he said huskily. She was viciously glad to hear some sign of emotion from him, even if it was only embarrassment making him sound so rasped and different. After all they had done to one another out here in the lying summer shadows he ought to pay some price for what he had done to her tonight.

'Of course we must,' she whispered as much to Flora with her gentle but stony smile as to Darius the almost-lover.

The goddess was a figment of the sculptor's imagination just as the Darius who wanted more from her than a stolen kiss must have been made up by hers. This man was not the one who had kissed her so urgently and wanted her so badly just moments ago. He coughed softly, as if to get her attention, and how could he not know how totally he had it already, the great fool? Every move he made, every furtive look he cast her was the centre of her attention even now he was rejecting her so coolly. Then he held out his arm to her, as if he was being polite to a distant acquaintance, as if he really was made of stone. How could he snuff out all traces of intimacy between them as if they were nothing to each other and maybe she had imagined it all?

'No, thank you,' she said stiffly and locked her hands together behind her back in a childish gesture she knew betrayed her agitation in the face of his coldness, but she could not touch him right now. It would cost more composure than she had available to lay even the tips of her fingers on his sleeve as if he meant no more to her than she must have done to him. 'Tell them I wanted to see more of the garden by moonlight and you lost me in the shadows. I will join you all again shortly and drink tea as if nothing untoward ever happened.'

'I am sorry,' he repeated like a gruff boy having an apology forced out of him by his elders.

'Don't be,' she said, stiffly offended now. *She made me*, she could almost hear his inner school-boy excusing himself. 'Oh, just go away,' she told him with a weary sigh and turned down one of the fairy-lit paths to get away from him and this ridiculous urge to grab him by the back of his neck and force him to stoop down again and kiss her to prove it had been every bit as much his fault as it was hers that she took fire in his arms, when he had obviously only been a little bit drunk and unable to resist trying his luck with any almost available woman.

She heard his whispered and rather more sincere sounding, 'Sorry,' waft after her and tears pricked her eyes. She shook her head without turning round and refused to cry over him. It felt as if something potentially precious had been stifled at birth and she wanted to mourn it for a few moments in the dark, but he was certainly not worth her tears.

Chapter Ten

Fliss was relieved when the impromptu party broke up half an hour or so after she returned to the terrace outside Mrs Corham's house, doing her best to pretend she had been communing with the brilliant stars practically ever since she and Mr Yelverton wandered away to look at roses, or whatever the others thought they had been doing in the scented darkness. They were deluded if they thought the night and the moon would make a romance bloom between correct Miss Grantham and reluctant Mr Yelverton. Instead it made her moon-mad and she was almost sure she regretted every minute of those kisses and that—whatever it had been. If he had not been so shamefaced and chastened she might not be either, but he was and he had spoilt so much she did not want to think about it until it no longer hurt and that seemed a very long time away. Now she had a dreadful headache and felt as if she had aged a few decades since she set out for that wretched party so full of dizzy anticipation of who knew quite what. It seemed impossible that was only a few hours ago as now a very different Fliss set out with a naive belief that tonight would be momentous for her in some undefined way.

Well, it was, Darius Yelverton had wanted her and she had wanted him, but he did not care, so it could never be more than a want, an urge to mate when the brake was taken off his chilly desire to wed money by that wretched punch. Yet she still felt as if a great weight of sorrow was pressing down on her as they bade one another a stiff goodnight and parted as if they hardly knew each other.

And it was true; they did not. They knew nothing about one another despite two dramatic meetings now and a furtive kiss in the dark that almost became more. He obviously had no idea what she felt and thought when they were locked in each other's arms like passionate lovers. She had not known how undone a man could be by a curious impulse and some mistaken matchmaking. But she did now. At the beginning of tonight she did not know how joyous and seductive and tempting a man's kisses could be in the moonlight, but she certainly did now. She knew why dark, scented corners must always be avoided without the presence of a stern duenna *and* that a man could want a woman with every fibre of his being one moment and be stiff and sorry and shocked about what they had nearly led themselves into the next.

Well, if he regretted those at the time enchanted moments in Flora's grotto he would never rue them as bitterly as she did. It would only have taken a faint promise to try to work out what it was that drew them together like stardust and champagne and she would be walking home on air, but he was not the sort of man to make such false promises to a single lady without a comfortable fortune. So she had been right all along: impulsive, passionate, all-consuming love was an emotion that ought never to be trusted. Even her parents had loved each other so much they could not endure being parted so they left her behind as soon as they decided she needed to learn to be a young lady instead of a sailor's brat.

So there you are then, Felicity, all that wild love they had for one another left you grief stricken and alone, but at least it was love.

And it turned out just the same for Marianne and her Daniel in the end; he was dead and Marianne had to endure so much grief and loneliness without him. Better never to love in the first place than be left alone all over again. And Mr Yelverton's passion for her had not even been anywhere close to love—it was a faint and fleeting thing that had left her hurt and aching and feeling less than she was before, rather than someone unique or special to him. Good, now she knew how it felt to meet the dark side of herself, she would know how best to avoid it in future. Lord Stratford had offered her a sensible and reasoned marriage of mutual convenience and from where she stood now that sounded wonderful. She could hardly wait for His Lordship to come home and begin the arrangements. If not for this appalling headache, she would probably be dancing for joy now Mr Yelverton had shown her the folly of longing for more than a rational marriage with a polite and rational lord would ever be able to offer her.

'I don't know what you did or said to make Miss Grantham so cold and distant with you. I was expecting icicles to form in the air when you said goodnight to each other just now,' Marianne said as they drove back to Owlet Manor by the light of a now rather weary-looking midsummer moon.

'We scarcely spoke two words to one another after you and your familiars pushed us out into the darkness to become better acquainted than either of us really want to be,' Darius said and he could hear the defensiveness in his own voice. He knew his sister was smiling sceptically and congratulating herself on the success of her insane scheme to throw him and Miss Grantham together. How could he get her to stop doing it without revealing that he felt as if he had trampled something rare and precious underfoot like a mannerless clod tonight? If he let Marianne see that he felt regretful and nostalgic about that bittersweet interlude in the rose garden, she would probably be delighted. Goodness knew why she was so intent on steering him towards any female without a decent marriage portion who crossed their path.

Not that many females did so in the deep country-side around Owlet Manor.

He could have met a bent old crone instead of a lush young beauty the other day and at least he would have been a lot happier about it now. Then his life would have stayed happily inside the routine they had fallen into since they came here to make a new life. He liked that steady life after the nomadic one he had led in the army. Knowing he would wake up tomorrow in the same place as he had the day before felt like balm to the damaged soul he did not know he still had until the fighting finally stopped. It was home and hope for him, his rundown but still-splendid inheritance. He felt a little ashamed that he loved the place so fiercely. They had only been here for a matter of weeks, but he knew he would do that decade of soldiering all over again to keep it if he had to, so marrying enough money to maintain and love it properly and dower his sisters ought not to feel like such a sacrifice.

'I am not sure I should be classed as a witch by my own brother, simply because I think you ought to spend more time with a true lady to remind you what it feels like.'

'I *knew* you disliked Mrs Frampton,' he said. 'You greeted the woman so coolly tonight you were only just on the right side of rude.'

'I can see nothing about her to like, not even her moneybags.'

'You might despise them, but I need money to

get our house in order and make the land and stock properly productive again. We need to buy a new ram to improve the bloodlines of both flocks and I want to keep cattle and maybe even breed horses as well. Then we must mend the barn roofs somehow and all that before we even begin on what we need for the house—I know you will have a list for that a mile long. We both know the old place is damp and anti-quated and full of moth-eaten tapestries and wormy old furniture that should have been thrown on the bonfire a century ago. It will cost a fortune to drag the place into this century.'

'Most of what I have found under the debris is perfectly good. With a few repairs and some careful cleaning a lot of it will be almost like new again. I had Isaac burn the most worm-ridden chairs and put white vinegar and lemon oil on the rest and on all the beams and the floor of the chapel so there will not be any more infestations for us to worry about.'

'The chapel has not been used for nearly a cen-tury, Nan. We have to be realistic about what we can save and what must be let go. Even if I do manage to raise enough money to modernise the main house and land somehow, we cannot do everything.'

'We will come about; you only need to be pa-tient. With all the hard work we are already putting into the house and your improvements on the farm everything is getting better already. I know we need to keep a sensible grasp on what can be done until the old place begins to pay for itself again, but there is no need for drastic measures, Darius. We are far better off now than we were six months ago, thanks to Great-Uncle Hubert, and I think you are forgetting you came home intending to find work of any sort you were offered rather than stay in the army and we both have a great deal more than that now.'

'There is not enough time to wait for a decent life to develop here for you and Viola before you are both worked half to death and old before your time.'

'I *beg* your pardon?' Marianne said in the ominous voice that had even made their illustrious commander-in-chief stop in his tracks on one memorable occasion back in Portugal. She knew how to leave it echoing into a stern silence and Darius was glad they were driving a placid plough horse instead of Nero, because he would have skittered and plunged and threatened to bolt if he was here to take exception to Mrs Turner's finest rebuke to the male of the species.

'Perhaps that was not very well put,' Darius admitted gruffly.

'Perhaps?'

'Very well then, it was not.'

'No, it certainly was not; nor was it properly thought out. I refuse to care if I am thought rough and unladylike for not sitting about with my smelling salts moaning about the state of your house instead of getting on and doing something about it by others, but I will not listen to my own brother expecting me to do so as well. Have you any idea how boring it is to sit around waiting to be polite to any visitors who deign to call and might even feel like being polite to Daniel's unrepentant widow today? I thought I was done with such flummery for good when we came here, but apparently you want me to do it here as well. At this very moment I am extremely tempted to make you get out of this gig and walk home, then find myself another position as a housekeeper as soon as possible.'

'I did not say you look old now, just that you and Viola might be a lot older than you are now before I can hope to make enough money to dower you properly. And we are only a couple of miles from home so I can easily walk the rest of the way,' he pointed out unwisely. It was his night for doing things he ought not, so why stop at kissing governesses?

'I dare say you will be quite comfortable in the cart shed when you get there, then,' she said abruptly and although he was bigger and stronger than she was she knew he would get out and walk home if she told him to and really meant it.

'I have slept in far worse places.'

'Yes, when you were young,' she said with a loud sniff.

'No, a matter of weeks ago in France, although I admit the army feels a world away now that we are here and nobody is shooting at me on a daily basis. Peace, sister dear?'

'Not if you truly mean to marry a fortune, especially not on mine and Viola's behalf. She would not want you to wed Mrs Frampton either. I shall move away and take up a position with whoever will have me if you are really going to be such an idiot and I would rather stay here. Viola and I prefer to be busy and she will probably disown you as well if you insist on marrying money for her sake so there will be no point in your sacrificing yourself for our sakes when neither of us will be here to watch you rue the day you wed for money.'

'Then I refuse to lose this place for my own sake as well, but I will not risk you two being homeless and penniless if anything happens to me.'

'It is not as if Owlet Manor is entailed and Daniel and I were often penniless when the Paymaster did not turn up in the Peninsula, but it never killed us,' Marianne said flatly.

'Maybe not, but it would destroy me if you had to live the narrow sort of life you endured with our parents in Bath ever again.'

'It is not Mama and Papa's fault we do not understand each other. If that is anyone's doing, it is mine for running away with Daniel in the first place, but I refuse to regret it, Darius. And I would far rather live with them again than see you trapped in an unhappy marriage.'

'But only think what a fool I would be if I risked losing Owlet Manor and the estate for the sake of an emotion I do not even believe in, Nan.'

'Living off your wife's money would be sheer torture for you in the end, Darius, and I cannot understand why you will not see it. Even Mama and Papa dote on each other, for all their differences. They would be horrified if they knew what you are so intent on doing to yourself.'

'I will never marry for love, so why not? I own a fine old house and a decent enough estate, so it is not as if she would be getting nothing for her money and she will be lady of the manor as well.' And he must never let his sister find out it was watching her being torn apart by grief after Daniel died that made him resolve not to risk such a catastrophe for his one-day wife. There was far less chance of him being hit with ball or grape shot, or spit through by a cavalry sabre or a lance nowadays, but life was uncertain and farming could be hazardous. Love was simply not for him, despite redheaded governesses who ought to be even more practical than he was trying to be. The sooner Miss Grantham went off to teach her next pupils and his sisters accepted how he felt about love and marriage not going together, the happier they would all be.

'If you are fool enough to wed Mrs Frampton, she will get a bargain she certainly does not deserve if you ask me, but that's the problem, isn't it? You never do ask me what I want when you are intent on rearranging my life for me without my knowledge or consent.'

'Because I know you will say put love first and worry about tomorrow when it comes.'

'Then I will be right, won't I?'

'You really think so even now, even after you lost Daniel so brutally?'

'Of course,' she said without a second thought. 'I knew he was a soldier when I married him so I was lucky to have him for as long as I did. If you ever fall in love, you might finally understand that a day, or even an hour, spent with the one you love is infinitely more worth having than a lifetime with someone you do not.'

'As well that I never intend to fall in love, then.'

'I pity you if that turns out to be true,' his sister said very seriously and they lapsed into silence for the rest of the journey.

There was no point in them talking when they were so firmly fixed on opposite sides of the argument that neither was willing to move. His sister thought the pain and grief that had turned her into a shadow of her true self for months after Daniel died was all worth it for the love they had shared. Darius disagreed profoundly; no attraction, shared humour, or mutual aims were worth her bitter suffering when Daniel was killed. Even now she had learned to hide it better he knew she missed her husband viciously most of the time. He was the one who had to watch her first terrible grief for Daniel *and* miss the glowing, laughing, passionate Marianne she was when she was married to his sergeant-major.

Locked up with pity for his sister was his own grief for his friend and brother-in-law and the guilt he still carried to this day, because Daniel had died at his side instead of him, the officer the sharp-shooter was really trying to kill. And in those terrible weeks after Badajoz Darius knew he could never put a woman through such abject misery. He still believed it was wrong to love someone without a thought for what tomorrow would bring and, as long as he kept away from complicated females like Miss Grantham, he should be able to guard them both from any further damage. Kissing her in the moonlight, feeling far too much for an impoverished lady in the shadows of an enchanted garden?

Honestly, Darius, what madness came over you tonight?

Thank heavens they woke up to what they were about to do in time. Another five or ten minutes and they would have been so deeply compromised they would have had to marry and make the best of a poor lot. Miss Felicity Grantham had had a very lucky escape tonight. He hoped she realised it and avoided dark corners and men like him from now on.

Chapter Eleven

It was all very well for Darius to decide he would avoid Miss Grantham in future, but Marianne seemed hell bent on making it impossible for him to pretend the redheaded temptress did not exist.

He shot his sister a warning glare when he found them sitting in the small parlour one morning when he came in from the fields after helping cut the last of the hay. The men were never truly comfortable when he ate with them, but how he wished he had stayed away and never mind embarrassing them. The distinctive gleam of Miss Grantham's copper-red curls in the sunlight made his heartbeat stutter, then race on as she sat there so intent on her sewing, yet so unique and vital in a shaft of sunlight from the open latticed window nearby it seemed wrong not to look at her and yearn. Even the sun seemed fascinated by the brightness of her hair and was highlighting every fierce strand with extra brightness so there was a depth and richness to the colour he had not let himself notice before.

Lucky he saw her first, then, before she realised he was here and staring at her like a dumbstruck fool, so there was no harm done. He muttered a brief hello in her general direction, said something gruff and ungainly about changing his shirt, then turned on his heel and strode away. Hopefully he would manage to compose himself while he was upstairs doing just that.

In his not-very-restored bedchamber he caught a glimpse of himself in the square of mirror he used for shaving and realised the rip in his shirt was even worse than he had thought. He should never have let himself become so fascinated by the play of sunlight on copper curls with fiery golden lights and rich chestnut depths in them that he forgot he was so unfit for her ladylike company, unfit for her in every way, he reminded himself sternly. Even as he searched for a clean and decent shirt to wipe out her impression of him as a barbarian home from the hunt his thoughts still lingered on that picture of Miss Felicity Grantham, so warm and vivid and alive in the shaft of sunlight she had probably only sat in so it would light up her sewing more clearly. Somehow he knew she would never deliberately put herself in the place where she would show to best advantage, so it could not have been a deliberate goad for him to look harder at what he had rejected the other night after those stupid, magical kisses.

He caught himself contrasting her natural dignity and good manners with Mrs Frampton's lack of both and even poor, awkward little Miss Pelham's puppy-like eagerness. One would drape herself in any pose that would attract masculine attention and the other would blush consciously and try to look away, half-pleased and half-terrified that her fortune was making her far more attractive to gentlemen like him than she might have been if she was penniless. Mrs Frampton would watch him with greedy eyes and let him know he owed her whatever she wanted because her money would be paying for it. He ripped off the torn and useless old shirt with an exclamation of disgust—not for the worn-out cloth, but his own revulsion with the grubby business of finding, courting, then marrying a wealthy bride. It would almost have been easier to carry on being Captain Yelverton than have this wonderful old house, three farms, two sisters and his elderly parents' welfare depending on him marrying a big enough fortune to make them all secure for the first time in decades.

Except he was sick of war and the stench and terror of the battlefield and deep down inside he knew he was done with fighting as soon as he heard the bittersweet news the war had been over before the bloody Battle of Toulouse began. If only the message had reached them sooner, it need never have happened; all those men need not have died or been mortally wounded on both sides for no reason at all. So now he must count his blessings and do everything he could to make his family secure because he was one of the ones who knew what poverty, invasion and insecurity truly looked like.

Now, where was he? Oh, yes, a clean shirt, he recalled as he frowned at the changes peace had made to his body. He was already brown from where he usually stripped off his shirt when it was soaked with sweat or getting in the way. There was muscle tight and heavy across his chest and shoulders and not even being on campaign had honed him to the peak of fitness he had got to now. He frowned at the sight of the newly healed wound across his left arm and older scars of battle on his body—a spent bullet had nicked his ribs, a lance slashed so close it would have killed him if Daniel had not pulled him back and away from the French cavalry charge in the nick of time. Darius felt tears sting his eyes at the thought of his brother-in-law and how much he owed him for saving his life more than once. He owed him Marianne's happiness and safety during their five years of marriage most of all. She was Daniel's world when all was said and done, so Darius must make sure she would never need to worry about where her next penny was coming from ever again, for his friend's sake as well as her own. There was his good reason to get on with real life and stop daydreaming about being rich and secure enough to marry whoever he pleased.

Little chance of Miss Grantham waiting for that fantasy to come true after the other night, when he pretended to be an idle rake who kissed vulnerable females in the dark for devilment and a frisson of frustrated desire. So why did he do it? Best not think about the answer to that question, best get on with whatever came next, just as he had been doing ever since he made himself turn away from her, and remember all the people whose happiness depended on him not shackling himself to a penniless governess.

Shirts, then—yes, keep thinking about shirts, Darius. A shortage of them is more important in your everyday life than the red-haired, dark-eyed pocket Venus currently sitting in the parlour sewing.

She and Marianne must think whatever it was they were doing was urgent for Marianne to sit still in the middle of the day, or had they simply been busying their fingers while they talked of this and that? He hoped he was not part of any *this* or *that* they had been discussing. Yet deep down, in the dark inner place that drew him into moonlit gardens and made him give in to a stupid urge to find out how Miss Grantham tasted and felt and needed, he wanted to know she had looked up and been as shocked and surprised and secretly delighted to see him as he was to find her in Marianne's parlour.

Shirts—she was here to help Marianne make shirts. And no wonder when he was breaking out of the one he was almost wearing when he appeared in the doorway of this very parlour just now. Through the aged linen he must have worn under his uniform all the way from Spain to France, and quite often since for it to become so thin and worn out and fragile, she had been able to see his honey-gold skin glistening with manly effort once again. Even after the few seconds she had been allowed in order to gaze up at him like a tongue-tied idiot before he shot away as if he had been ambushed by hostile forces, she could see that his torso was as sun-kissed as his bare neck under that torn and revealing shirt. He certainly did not wear that wreck of a garment all the time; he could not do so and manage to be so tanned and satin-skinned over those work-hardened muscles of his. Her inner idiot longed to explore him bare-chested and as eager for her touch as she was to touch him, but that was just a silly fantasy.

Then she wondered how he had managed to wear out any of his shirts since he obviously did not wear them very much. Next she caught herself imagining him swinging a scythe or wielding a rake without one and looking so muscular and masculine it was probably as well Owlet Manor had no dairymaids to be distracted from their work by the sight of their employer striding about the place half-naked. Jealousy of non-existent young women who were sure to lust after such a masculine and muscular gentleman from a distance if they were here to watch him with hungry eyes was completely ridiculous.

She had not wanted to come here and risk meeting him after he had kissed her, then walked away as if she meant nothing to him but a moonlit mistake, but she could hardly make shirts for an unrelated male in Miss Donne's parlour instead of his. Her old friend would have been sure to ask who the outsized and obviously masculine garment was meant for and she could hardly claim a mythical male relative when Miss Donne knew she was only on distant terms with her uncle and her only male cousin, who probably had their shirts made in some haughty establishment for the nobility. It had made sense for her to come here with Marianne and carry on helping with the huge pile of sewing waiting for the odd few minutes when her friend was not frantically busy elsewhere. Fliss was better at plain sewing than intricate repairs to ancient and precious textiles, so she took over the seams of this sturdy cotton replacement for Mr Yelverton's old shirt while Marianne did more delicate work. Now she could see he really did need more new shirts than his sister had time to make him, but maybe this one would be different. Maybe her silly obsession with his fine muscular form and handsome face would end up sewn into the very fabric of it by the time she finished. Would he feel a little frisson of nostalgia and a faint thread of need whenever he put it on?

Oh, yes, she really hoped he would. She wanted him to be torn and tortured by the memory of something special and wonderful he had trampled underfoot as well as her. Maybe it was wrong of her, but she needed him to regret her when he found out she had the money to put his farm in good order and mend his roof and he had whistled her down the wind. She hoped he stung with frustration and nostalgia when he read about her betrothal to Lord Stratford in the morning papers once that impeccable gentleman was back in England for her to engage herself to. Was she really going to say yes to the Viscount, then? Probably, since she had met a man she could have loved and wanted quite ridiculously for the rest of her life and he had turned away from her as if those wondrous moments under the stars in Mrs Corham's garden meant nothing to him at all. Just as well she had not let herself tumble all the way into love with him then.

Much better if she concentrated on sewing the cotton cloth under her fingers and forgot who she was making it for. But she had lost the easy rhythm of her stitches now and almost stabbed herself with the needle when she thrust it so viciously through the sturdy stuff maybe she secretly wanted to stick it in him for being such a fool. Now look what he had done; she had never been a violent person, but today she badly wanted to shock or shake him into seeing everything he had thrown away the other night and make him realise he was a fool if he thought a fortune would make up for true friendship and deep feelings inside a marriage.

He had been a little bit too obvious in his survey of the Assembly Room that night, had he not? Maybe word had already got about that he needed to wed a fortune for Mrs Frampton to have watched him with such explicitly buying eyes across the dance floor while he measured her against his criteria for marriage. She shuddered at the idea of any woman thinking she had bought and paid for the man she was about to marry and decided, yes, Lord Stratford's offer sounded very tempting indeed. With wealth on both sides at least neither of them would ever need to fear they had been married for their money, even if they did not do it for love either.

'You told me your brother was busy in the fields today,' she said abruptly and bent over her sewing as she listened for Mr Yelverton's tread on the ancient stairs; so she could avoid seeing him again, obviously. He would not come back in here now he knew she was in the house. Even she knew enough about men to be sure he would not want any reminders of the disastrous mistake he so nearly made the other night. Mortifying to be merely one of those to him when it had felt so right being kissed and caressed by Darius Yelverton in the heat of the moment. And the less she thought about him and his glorious, fickle kisses, the better.

'He is,' Marianne replied earnestly, so Fliss must be wrong about her new friend scheming to throw them together. 'He hopes they can finish mowing and begin turning the hay today while the weather holds. He must have come in to get another shirt and snatch something to eat and drink while he was about it.'

So Marianne could not have known her brother would come back here in the middle of the day. Fliss felt guilty about thinking her new friend had planned their latest encounter after the bitter failure of her last scheme to throw them together. 'Oh, I see,' she said and felt herself blush at the memory of her fascinated survey of the man half-naked in the doorway just now, when he had only come into the house for a whole shirt. She bent over the cloth in her hands as if concentrating very hard and willed that betraying flush to die down. It was a curse being born red-headed and blushing like a peony at the drop of a hat was almost the worst part of it.

'Excuse me, I had best go and find him some food and make his tea, before he turns my pantry upside down searching for what he wants,' Marianne said, getting to her feet with a long-suffering sigh. 'He can eat it in the kitchen, since I doubt he will change everything else he has on when he intends to go out to work again. Darius knows full well I will not have him in here in his dirt now I have managed to get this room properly clean and tidy—when it is not full of my sewing, of course. Thank goodness you are a friend rather than one of Darius's nosy neighbours, though, for it is not fit for them to inspect as yet.'

Fliss shot her a quick smile to say *Thank you for not standing on ceremony with me*, then stared down at her sewing as Marianne left the room at much the same time Fliss could hear her brother coming down the stairs. At least Marianne was standing in the doorway this time so neither he nor Fliss could see one another and that proved Marianne was not plotting to throw them together any more. Good, she did not want to see how he looked in clean shirt sleeves and it was hardly gentlemanly of him to go about without a waistcoat or a cravat, even if it was a hot day and he intended to go back to his labours in the fields as soon as he had eaten. She imagined him sitting at the wide scrubbed table in the kitchen without that cravat and frowned down at the row of very wobbly stitches she had just set. She clicked her tongue in annoyance and pulled the needle from the thread so she could undo what ought never to have been done in the first place. Would she could undo his kiss from her memory at the same time, but the truth was she had been far too busy fantasising over this garment's future owner to pay much attention to her stitching. And it seemed he was so fast in her thoughts she could not unpick them and get that picture of him ardent and wanting her back the other night out of her silly head.

And what a little rabbit she was to sit here, feeling so flustered by his presence she could not even sew in a straight line. He was the one who had pulled away from her as if he had no idea why he had kissed such a quiz the other night. He was the one who ought to be ashamed of himself, not shrugging all that shame off on to her. She saw no good reason to go on sitting here as if she was the one who had led him into sinfully tempting places she had no idea existed until she met him. She undid the unsteady stitches, eyed the line that needed to be done again

and decided she was not going to let him make her
so timid and afraid of life that she hid in here cring-
ing while he ate and drank and took his ease a few
yards away.

She stood up, determined to prove she was still
herself, still Miss Felicity Grantham, one-time governess and a lady of independent means and determined character. An independent lady who refused
to cower in here because a gentleman had kissed her
as if she was crucial to his continued well-being, then
pretended he hardly knew her minutes later. Well, he
didn't know her if he thought she was going to pretend to be invisible because they were embarrassed
about what they did in the dark the other night. She
folded her sewing neatly, taking care to make sure
the needle was left on the outside, so not even Mr
Yelverton could sit on it and risk being stabbed in
the nether regions if she decided never to set another
stitch in his wretched shirt or come anywhere near
his dusty old house ever again.

He could have shaved before he intruded on them
as well. Taking off his work boots and sneaking
about the place in his stockings was bad enough,
but appearing all rough and redolent of hard work
and fresh air while he did so was much worse. His
stubble was lighter than his golden-brown and brutally cropped hair as well, so there had been a sort of
golden haze about his face as he stood in the doorway, looking horrified to see her sitting in his sister's
favourite parlour sewing his shirt. Well, he was about

to see her again whether he liked it or not. She sighed at her own folly in noticing so much about him in the short space of time he was standing in the doorway and gathered her courage before she plonked back down in her chair and set stitches again like a good little housewife.

'Even sewing feels like thirsty work today, so could I trouble you for some tea please, Marianne?' she asked from the kitchen doorway. She was brave, but not quite brazen enough to stroll boldly into the room, then sit down and wait for a cup of tea to appear on the scrubbed kitchen table in front of her.

'Of course, do come in and sit down and I will see if I can find a proper cup and saucer for you to drink it out of.'

'Thank you. And how do you do today, Mr Yelverton?' Fliss managed to say casually as she sat on a stool as far away from him as she could get, so he could sit back down on his, get on with his midday snack, then bolt for the fields again to avoid her. Her heartbeat jarred at her first sight of him again, then settled to a faster rhythm than usual, despite her airy resolution not to let him affect her in any way.

'I am very well, I thank you, Miss Grantham, and how do you do?'

'Oh, I am perfectly well, too,' she said and she was, or would be—when he had gone away again.

'Good,' he said and seemed lost for any more polite conversation.

Maybe she ought not to have come in here so

boldly after all. It might have been better to set a sternly even row of stitches in his wretched shirt and get it finished as fast as possible, then resolve to avoid his dangerous company and lie to her friend next time Marianne wanted a shirt made and Miss Donne was curious about her sewing.

'The—' she said, intending to talk about the weather or something equally neutral now she was here and wondering if it was such a good idea to face her demons after all.

'How—?' her handsomest demon said at the same time.

They both fell silent and waited for the other to begin some awkward comment about the heat or the time of year or how many beans made five, but luckily Marianne came back in and saved them the trouble.

'There you are; do pour Miss Grantham some tea, Darius. You are closest to the pot and I am busy.'

Fliss stared at the finely made Chinese porcelain handle-less cup in its bowl-like saucer and supposed they were left over from some lady of the manor's best tea set from many years ago, when a long-dead lady of Owlet Manor had genteel visitors to tea so they could be suitably impressed by the imported luxuries she could afford and they probably could not.

'That old thing has no handle, Nan; Miss Grantham will burn her fingers,' the master of it said quite gently and got up to fetch a smaller mug than his vast one

from the Welsh dresser nearby. He filled it with tea
and put it in front of Fliss, then passed over the milk
jug before sitting down again as if he could not drink
his own tea and get back to the real business of the
day fast enough.

'No, no sugar for me, thank you,' she told him as
he recalled his manners long enough to put down his
own mug of tea and raise a questioning eyebrow at
the nearby sugar bowl.

Marianne came back to the table with a huge
plateful of cold pie and cheese and pickles and some
fresh salad leaves she must have fetched in from the
garden earlier and set it before her brother. 'I should
have thought of that before I brought it in,' she said
with a rueful nod at the unused cup, 'but it is so delicate and finely made it seems a shame not to use it
when we have polite company.'

'Well, either fine ladies in olden days had iron fingers or they slurped their tea out of the saucer and I
cannot see Miss Grantham being comfortable doing
that,' her brother said as if he had found a neutral
subject of conversation and was going to cling to it
like a drowning man.

'I suppose they must have done something of the
sort, although it doesn't sound like very good manners,' his sister replied with a shrug to say it was
that old china curiosity or an earthenware mug and
at least she had tried.

'Best add a modern tea set to your vast shopping
list, Nan, and it seems as well the Drawing Room is

next on your list of places to be cleansed, repainted and reborn. When you have a fit place to receive them in we will be able to entertain our callers in far more style,' he persisted after a few bites of his luncheon and a hunted look at them blandly drinking their tea, as if he felt like an animal being fed for the benefit of spectators.

'I doubt they keep much choice of fine china in Broadley,' Marianne said discouragingly.

Fliss refused to notice his implication she was a visitor who refused to remain in the one room where polite company could be received as formally as the house could be formal in its current state. She had a suspicion her friend was in two minds about company so refined they could not join her in her little parlour or sit at the kitchen table like Fliss was doing as well. Of course there were sure to be a few snobbish local ladies who would look down their noses at the widow of a common soldier receiving guests in whatever room had been cleared of the lumber and dust of half a century lately, but there were a great many more who would come to visit out of curiosity and stay to be pleased that Mrs Turner was a lady of character and considerable charm, when she chose to exert it. Once word of Mr Yelverton's fine form, handsome face and a fine old house and estate to go with him got about they would come to see for themselves and most were very unlikely to risk offending him by giving his sister the cold shoulder. Anyway, Fliss could not refuse to come to Owlet Manor again and let Marianne think she considered herself too good to keep a soldier's widow company—even if she had been sewing her brother's dratted shirt all morning and that should prove her friendship well enough to excuse her.

'Then we must go to Worcester, since that's where they make the stuff,' he said as if determined his sister would not have any more excuses to put off callers now word would have got around they were clearing and cleaning this grand old house room by room and surely the drawing room must be high on the list?

'Maybe we could go when you are not quite so busy,' Marianne said as if she hoped to put off a visit to that venerable cathedral city as long as possible and receiving the local gentry even longer.

Marianne obviously thought her brother was being extravagant as well as interfering when there were so many other things they could spend money on first. Fliss felt uneasy as she listened to them carefully avoid asking one another what enough bone china for a gentleman's table and a lady's afternoon tea-drinking might cost. It was a novelty for her to be so much richer than those around her and she was not too sure that she liked it at the moment.

'You could make an outing of it,' Mr Yelverton persisted. 'Miss Donne is sure to know what kind of ware would be best suited to our purposes and how much of it we will need. She would be the perfect chaperon for you and Miss Grantham—if you are still here when I finally manage to persuade my stubborn sister it is necessary for us to make our visitors welcome and not a luxury, Miss Grantham.'

Miss Grantham nodded distantly and hoped she looked politely non-committal about the whole idea. In other circumstances it might have been fun to shop for this fine old house and maybe buy some of the gloves Worcester was famous for as well while they were over there. As a trip Marianne did not want to go on for goods she did not want to buy and thought they could not afford, it would feel uncomfortable to accompany her friend with the secret knowledge of her own fortune to struggle with the whole time. And Fliss did not see why she and Miss Donne should go in his stead when it was his house he was insisting on buying china for anyway.

'Maybe we could go in the autumn when the crops are safely in and the fat lambs have been sold,' Marianne said as if the longer she could put it off the better.

'Before then, Nan; we will have to be ready to receive any guests who have ventured all the way out here to pay their respects long before that.'

'They will be here to visit you, not me, and you are never in,' Marianne said flatly and Fliss's heart went out to her.

She could only imagine how her friend must have felt when she came back to England after her husband was killed to face everything from outright condemnation to tactless remarks about it being unfortunate she had lowered herself to marry such a

man, of course, but at least she was now free of him.
No wonder Marianne did not want to face any more
foolish prattle like that, but this was a very different
place and Fliss suspected Mrs Corham's influence
was enough to stop the worst of the gossip if she approved of Mr Yelverton's widowed sister.

'Both Miss Donne and Mrs Corham will want to
see how you are getting on with making this fine old
house clean and tidy and comfortable again before
the summer is out, Marianne,' Fliss said gently. She
had been determined to stay out of their argument,
but the need to reassure her friend that at least two
ladies would come here with only the best of intentions proved too much for her.

'And where Mrs Corham goes her wide circle of
friends will surely follow,' Mr Yelverton added clumsily and almost undid her good work.

She shot him a furious look and fought an urge
to pat Marianne's hand and say *There, there* when
she saw her pale at the idea of crowds of unwanted
visitors turning up on her doorstep in those two ladies' footsteps. 'If she tells them you are not ready
to receive visitors just yet, they will listen to her,
Marianne, but sooner or later they will come. You
are a gentleman's daughter and Mr Yelverton's sister and, as he is lord of the manor here, they will be
eager to meet you both.'

'I still married Daniel and I will never be ashamed
of him as they will expect me to be.'

'And the better sort of people will respect you for

that. Those who do not are not the kind you will want to mix with anyway, so they do not matter, do they?'

Marianne thought about what Fliss had said for a few moments. 'True,' she said at last and Mr Yelverton nodded approvingly. He wisely went on with his luncheon in determined silence and did not add his fourpennyworth this time. There was still that visit to Worcester to endure, though, and she wondered if she could find a convincing reason not to go as she sipped her tea and waited for him to go away again. She would feel even more of a fraud if she had to pretend not to be able to afford even a silver teaspoon when she could probably buy up a factory full of them and what would Marianne think of her for keeping such a secret when she found out? Never mind what her brother thought, he would probably ask her to marry him on the spot and pour her thirty thousand pounds into his empty coffers. Being his wife, bearing his children only because she had enough money to improve his house and land and dower his sisters would make his magical-seeming kisses and fiery passion a hair shirt for her. So what luck she had a very good offer from Lord Stratford to accept and he was a genuinely good man in need of a wife.

Chapter Twelve

Over the next couple of weeks Fliss managed to avoid visiting Marianne and Owlet Manor at times when she thought the master of the house might be in or working close by. She told herself she would prefer to stay away altogether, but the wicked Fliss he had revealed to her that night in Mrs Corham's shadowy garden enjoyed the frisson of delicious danger that shot through her whenever she caught a glimpse of Darius Yelverton going about his business in the distance. One morning Bad Fliss eyed him hungrily and furtively as Marianne drove past the field where he and his men were doing something with the sheep she did not even begin to understand. And he should be forced to cover his bare, suntanned back when any susceptible females were anywhere near him to see it. She did not want any other ones to watch the play of his work-honed muscles and the strength and suppleness of him with greedy eyes as he flipped a reluctant ewe backwards and held her still while someone else did whatever they had to do to the animal. Fliss's inner hussy whispered how delicious it might be to be near naked with him. Perhaps she could lie against his muscular torso and strong legs instead of an ungrateful sheep. His farmhands and any other nosy spectators would have to go, of course, and she thought she had wild and willing-to-stray Fliss under control again at last, but she was wrong. Now she was impatient with her inner self for thinking of him in such a shameless way when pride should forbid it even if good taste did not.

She wished Lord Stratford would hurry up and come home so they could begin the preparations for their marriage as soon as possible. While she admired and respected the Viscount, she did not long for him with a wickedly sweet and heady yearning deep inside her secret self that refused to go away however often she told it to. Dozens of pristine young ladies of impeccable breeding and good fortune would be ecstatic to receive such a flattering offer from the deliciously handsome, self-assured and delightfully rich Viscount Stratford. Yet warmth only spread through her at the fantasy of Mr Yelverton wanting and loving her as he was transformed into the perfect lover once he realised she was crucial to his continued well-being and to hell with money and marrying an heiress.

She almost reached out a betraying hand towards his oblivious back, then had to pretend she was batting away a fly. Luckily Marianne was so intent on her driving she did not seem to have noticed the long and hungry look Fliss had just cast her brother as they passed by. Somehow Fliss had to stop herself longing for him, so she turned her eyes to the front and gazed at the hills behind Owlet Manor until this dratted blush had died down and she was calm again.

It did not augur well for her marriage to another man that she could not get Darius Yelverton out of her head. If Lord Stratford stood in front of her right now, she would probably say no to him for that very reason, but she must consider those dark times when she awoke in the middle of the night and felt so desperately lonely as she asked herself if this was all she was ever going to have and it was not enough. She wanted children of her own and Lord Stratford's businesslike proposal could be her only chance of marriage to a good and trustworthy man and a family. At times like that she felt lonely to the bone at the thought of never having a husband and children and at least Lord Stratford respected her. They might even learn to love one another in time, if they worked hard at their marriage.

Mr Yelverton did not want to marry her, or maybe he would when he knew about her money, but that was not a good enough reason to agree. She might look like the perfect wife for him if he found out she had money, but Lord Stratford was the one who had made her an honest proposal. She could marry him for the sake of children and companionship and, as his acres and houses were all in prime condition and not in the least need of her money, he was a rare if not unique suitor for her hand.

'I am going to make you a gown, Marianne,' she said to distract herself from the endless dilemma of what to do about her future.

'I doubt if the spiders and sheep will appreciate it,' Marianne joked, but Fliss sensed unease under the light-hearted manner and wondered if Marianne thought she would be betraying her dead husband if she dressed well now he was not here to appreciate it.

'You need something fine and frivolous to make you feel better after a hard day's work, even if only the sheep and your brother are present to see you wearing it. Those bolts of cloth you found in the sea chest in that quaint little bedchamber up in the attics look promising to me and Miss Donne will help us with the cutting and fitting of it. It should not cost more than a few pennies for thread and trimmings, if that is what you are worrying about.'

'No, it is not that, but I really do not want to be noticed as a woman now, Fliss. I shall never marry again and it would be a waste of effort for you to even try to make me look like an idle lady who sits about her brother's house waiting for polite company to call, because I am my brother's housekeeper and I do not have the time or the inclination to be called on.'

'Then wear it in private, when you want to feel elegant and feminine again after a hard day's work and a good long soak in a scented bath. We do not intend to hold you at gunpoint while we fit it on you, but I am quite sure Miss Donne will think of a way to keep you still without her having to resort to force.'

'Better if you helped me make curtains out of all the bolts of fabric that are still useable as I intended.'

'Not for those of us who have to look at you it isn't,' Fliss joked and was relieved when Marianne laughed and even seemed slightly excited at the prospect of having a new gown or two to wear when they looked through the lengths of cloth laid up goodness knew how many years ago with an eye to what suited her, rather than the bedroom or reception room she had in mind to make good next.

'Thank you, Miss Grantham,' Darius Yelverton said quietly from behind her and Fliss nearly jumped out of her skin.

She had been taking a stroll through what remained of the pleasure gardens next to the old moat at Owlet Manor and dreaming of times gone by and who planted it all and how did they feel when they sauntered through the neat walkways and finely trimmed topiary the wildness around her hinted at here and there. Her eyes had needed a change after another morning of fine sewing, but this time at least she was making Marianne's new gown instead of his shirts, so she could not imagine why he had startled her with his abrupt words when he had been avoiding her so carefully all this time. And it felt too much like him thanking her in the moonlight as they made their

way back to Mrs Corham's garden after the rowdi-
ness of the midsummer ball more than a fortnight
ago now. She did not need a reminder of that night
either. 'What are you thanking me for, Mr Yelverton?' she said stiffly.

'Helping my sister live again,' he said simply and
sincerely and how could she think up a flippant reply
now?

'Marianne is a good friend and has done as much
for me as I have for her.'

'I agree she is a wonderful person, but you have
given us so much time and effort for no reward and
now you are making Marianne a new gown, so I
would say the balance is very much in our favour,'
he said and why did he have to be so dangerously
attractive when he was being so open about his love
for his family?

'You clearly have no idea of the life a governess
leads, Mr Yelverton,' she said a little sharply because
she could not let herself soften towards him and lay
herself open to such hurt ever again.

'No, my life has been very different to yours and
I am the wrong sex, of course, so what is your life
like when you are teaching?'

'Constrained,' she said, uncomfortable with the
subject she had raised now and wishing he would
go away again.

'So is the life of an officer, but probably not by
the same things.'

'Certainly mine is not as dangerous, but I am sure

you never had to look far for company, what with so many other officers around you and in the same situation. A governess is isolated from the family who employ her because she is an upper servant and the other servants usually resent her. It can be a very lonely life, so of course I value your sister's friendship when I have often yearned for such a staunch friend of my own age, Mr Yelverton.'

'Aye, Marianne is true as steel. I hope you liked your pupils, though—even I can see that would help make such a narrow life seem more bearable,' he said and looked as if he worried about his other sister now she followed her late occupation.

When Fliss thought of some of the rumours she had heard of governesses seduced and deserted by unscrupulous men in the households where they worked she could hardly blame him for trying so hard to free his little sister from the chance of loneliness and exploitation. Yet if Miss Yelverton was anything like Marianne Fliss could not imagine her being taken in by such a rogue.

'Luckily Juno, my latest charge, is a dear girl and excellent company when she forgets her diffidence,' she said and at least she could tell the truth about that.

'You sound as if you grew very fond of her,' he said.

Fliss realised she was smiling at the thought of her former pupil's lively curiosity and the quiet sense of humour under all that paralysing shyness. 'Yes, and that is another frustration of being a governess. As soon as Juno was old enough to be launched into society I was dismissed and she is very unhappy and I cannot help her.'

'It must be hard to be so important in a girl's life one moment and surplus to requirements the next,' he said as if he was trying to understand such a very different life from his own. That felt rather endearing of him and she could not stop having this conversation and walk away somehow when all the different facets of this complicated man fascinated her. 'You had a governess yourself once upon a time, though, did you not?' he asked next and she should have walked away before this got more personal. 'Why did you follow in Miss Donne's footsteps if your family were wealthy enough to have you educated by such a fine and learned lady?'

'My uncle took me in when I was orphaned and allowed me to share lessons with his own daughter, despite still being furious with my mother for marrying against his wishes. He made it very clear I was not welcome under his roof even so and when my cousin was ready to make her debut in polite society he told me it was high time I earned my own living. As I had received such an excellent education, his sister had already found me a place as a nursery governess.'

'If you are the same age as your cousin, you must have been very young.'

'I was seventeen, but I always knew my uncle

only took me in on sufferance. I was glad to get away from his cold charity once Miss Donne had gone and I had decided I might as well make the best of things and teach my very reluctant pupils to the best of my ability.'

'It does not sound like an easy post for a young governess.'

'No, it was a challenge but I suppose I must have done well enough at it since the boys' mother recommended me to Juno's grandmother when the last of her sons went off to his preparatory school and we all sat back to count our grey hairs.'

'I cannot see any,' he said with a lingering glance at her ridiculous hair as if it fascinated him.

Unlikely, she told herself sternly. 'Nevertheless that is the story of my employment so far,' she said and at least that was true, even if she was a lady of means now and facing a very different future. 'How did *you* feel about going off to war at much the same age I took to teaching spoilt boys their letters, Mr Yelverton?'

'Uncertain,' he said with a rueful grin that made her regret not knowing the engaging boy he must have been before war armoured him against her and the world. 'My parents assumed I would follow my father's footsteps to Oxford then prepare for ordination. Needless to say I disagreed but the only alternative to the church was the army or navy and I have always preferred dry land.'

'I am trying to imagine you as an earnest young

clergyman,' she said and shook her head because it was impossible; there was nothing of the stooped scholar or hell-and-brimstone preacher about him.

He was too honed and sceptical after his life on campaign to be anything of the sort. She could imagine him at seventeen, full of dash and daring and far too impulsive and idealistic. Then she thought of his first battle and her heartbeat jarred at the danger and dreadfulness he must have faced that day. The boy in him must have been revolted by the stench of blood and gunpowder and fear and all without very much idea of what was going on beyond his small corner of the field. She could only imagine his shock and horror as men fought and died around him, after a boyhood of school and whatever tranquil country village his father had ministered to at the time. He must have been terrified and she had to admire him for not running away. Heaven forbid he ever realised it, but she pitied that reluctantly brave and probably homesick lad. She wished more of him survived in the man, so he might look harder at what he was doing as he stood here trying to take a polite interest in his sister's new friend. He was denying himself the power and depths of his own feelings and never mind the ruthless logic he brought to bear on his inheritance. He might let himself love her for the sheer pleasure and promise of it, if only he was less hardened by loss and all those years of doing his duty. But then again, he might not. He could really have been carried away by adulterated punch and heady summer darkness on the night that still yawned between them as they stood here being politely interested in one another's lives as if they had only just met.

'I would have been a terrible vicar,' he said and shook his head at the very idea, as if he was not worthy to follow his father's chosen path.

Without having met the reverend gentleman she could not say if it was a saintly one, but she sensed depths in Mr Darius Yelverton that went way beyond his father's limited experience of love and life. The great idiot was doing his best to ignore them and she felt a tug of exasperated affection for him, despite his stubbornness. He thought himself such a bad man now, but Marianne had said enough about their life in the Duke of Wellington's army to make Fliss realise he was respected and admired by most of his men, apart from the hard little knot her friend claimed plagued every army with drunkenness and greed for plunder. And his sister was so very proud of him as well. Marianne had been a sergeant's wife and would know if her brother was the lazy and self-serving officer he pretended.

'I should imagine quite a lot of vicars do as well,' she said mildly. 'Do you regret not taking that road now, though?'

He frowned as if he was looking back over impossible distances at the boy he was then. 'No,' he said, shaking his head as if there was no way back to that sort of innocence. 'Better a poor officer than an inadequate priest.'

'Perhaps you expect too much of yourself,' she defended him against what she sensed were impossibly high standards he had set himself as leader, counsellor and protector of the men under his command, even if he did demand loyalty and obedience from them in return.

'As a poor officer or a failed priest?' he asked.

'There you are, you see, you are doing it again.'

'How very tedious of me,' he said wearily.

'Yes, it is. You did not fail as a priest because you refused to even consider becoming one, so how could you? And from what your sister says you were a brave and conscientious officer and your men loved you. You put care of them before your own comfort and I may not know much about battles and marches and the rest of the duties and tedium of a soldier's life on the march, but I do know a man's true colours could not remain hidden for long, so you did not fail as an officer or a man.'

'I did—my best friend and brother-in-law died instead of me at Badajoz, Miss Grantham. He was shot through the head because he moved the wrong way at the wrong moment and took the bullet meant for me.'

'And you arranged all that on purpose, did you?'

'No, of course not, even I am not quite vain enough to believe it was my doing. Thank God I did not know it was coming my way and dodge behind him or I would never have been able to look my sister in the face again without flinching.'

'So you are right, then, you would have made a

very poor clergyman if you questioned the ways of God that night and sound as if you have been doing so ever since.'

'I am not even sure I believe in Him any more since Dan died beside me and I could do nothing to save him,' he said shortly and frowned at the moorhen chiding its mate on the lake as if it was their fault he still felt so raw and on edge about his brother-in-law's death. 'He was a far better man than I will ever be.'

'I think you would surprise yourself if you stayed still long enough to catch up with who you really are, Mr Yelverton.'

'And a more cryptic comment I have rarely heard, Miss Grantham. You are the oddest governess I have ever encountered.'

'How many of us have you met?'

'My younger sister; Miss Donne and you,' he listed as if that was enough.

'Not many to judge us by, then.'

'Oh, I don't know; all three of you are extraordinary in your own way.'

'And you are very adept at changing the subject, sir. I suppose you learnt that in the army as well.'

'No, that was from having two little sisters who always seemed to think they knew better than I did while we were growing up,' he said with a boyish grin that made her hope there was more of the idealistic young man who had gone off to war than he thought still there under his protective shell. 'Speaking of whom, here is Marianne in search of one of us.'

'That will be you, I suspect, since I have never met anyone so reluctant to be fitted with a new gown so she would not seek me out to make her try it on again.'

'Nevertheless, I am sincerely grateful to you for making it and for perhaps getting her to realise she is part of the wider world around here instead of simply my housekeeper and dear sister.'

'I think accepting that part of her new life is for her to do one day, but I am glad you think I might have helped,' Fliss said and turned to greet her friend with a serene smile that gave the lie to the tumult he had woken up inside her all over again.

Chapter Thirteen

Today she had let herself see the damage war had done him under that trick he had of turning back into self-contained Captain Yelverton again whenever his emotions threatened to get out of hand. But even if she could see it there was nothing she could do to help him heal when he was determined this defiant spark of connection between them from the first moment they set eyes on each other would go out if they ignored it stubbornly enough. Well, she would be stubborn as well then. She was determined to get Marianne's new gown finished before Lord Stratford came to find out her answer to his perplexing question and news of her fortune leaked out. And it was high time she moved on with her life now. Miss Donne had been very kind and welcoming and had kept her secrets when it was in her nature to be open and honest. It must have troubled her to do so. She must want to be alone again in her own little house with her dog and her maidservant and her garden to keep her busy. Her dearest and oldest friend ought to have the peace and quiet she so richly deserved after all those years of teaching other people's children for a living.

And Fliss could tell Miss Donne was concerned about her own restlessness as well as her decision to wed a nobleman without even a smidgeon of love between them. She suspected her friend knew she was not sleeping properly and that she felt deeply unsure of herself as a woman now that the man who plagued her dreams and ruined her sleep had kissed her so passionately, then coolly walked away as if they were mere acquaintances. Her impulsive side, the one that went about kissing strange men in moonlit gardens, wanted to rail at him for doing that and demand he regretted what might have been as well. Everyday Fliss still managed to keep a guard on her tongue and not argue with him. And how was a woman to show him the error of his ways if he would not even let her close enough to show him there was a better road to follow? She could hardly challenge him out loud when he was so determined there was nothing personal between them. Still, she obviously meant nothing to him, so she could hardly order him to come to his senses and realise what a wretched life he was heading for if he did not put feelings before hard logic.

Time rolled on despite her resolution to be gone as soon as she could. She could hardly leave when Lord

Stratford was stubbornly absent and she wondered if she ought to employ a chaperon for herself and embark on a tour of the Lakes or some such adventure while she waited for the Viscount to come back and claim her as a prospective wife. If she agreed. Here Fliss still felt as if Marianne and Miss Donne were conducting a sly campaign to throw her and Mr Yelverton together at every turn and it was like scraping away at a wound that refused to heal. She told herself she would have felt uncomfortable with him knowing what they were up to even if they had never kissed like lovers and parted as strangers.

Even when the first gown was done and declared perfect for Marianne by everyone except Marianne, Fliss felt she had to help her new friend with her mountains of sewing and mending. It would feel wrong to sit on her hands in Broadley while Marianne worked from dawn to dusk on that neglected and dusty old house, then sat down in the evening to start on her sewing. Working on another gown, from a carefully rolled piece of shimmering silk velvet Mr Yelverton had discovered before his sister could find it in a dusty trunk in the farm office, felt like a secret she did not entirely want to share with a man who still eyed her as if she might be dangerous. Still, it gave her and Miss Donne something constructive to do in the long summer evenings when there was no performance at the little theatre in town or a private dinner to go to, or simply an evening with one of Miss Donne's many friends. And Fliss could see

Marianne looking dramatic and confident and beautiful in the exquisitely made stuff if she could ever be persuaded to wear it. The rich brown stuff was undershot with golden undertones much like those in Marianne's hair and her bright blue eyes would seem all the more striking with such a foil to echo the colours in her hair.

So, one overcast and uncertain-looking morning, she eyed the latest panel of the half-made gown that needed to be delicately and perfectly matched to the next and wondered if it was a good idea to set out for Owlet Manor today. From the look of the lowering clouds and mist-shrouded hills she could be faced with a journey back in the pouring rain, or have to spend the day cooped up there with the master of the house pacing its ancient halls in frustration because nothing could be done outside and she was inside them stopping him settling to anything else. She decided no, it was not worth it, not even to finish his latest shirt and know Marianne had a supply of them ready so she need not labour on at them once Fliss had gone off to marry her Viscount—if her Viscount still wanted to marry her, of course. She was still brooding on His Lordship's offer and her willingness to accept it when she was so ridiculously attracted to another man. Look what Darius Yelverton had turned her into now—a dishonest woman.

'Message for you, Miss Grantham,' Miss Donne's maidservant broke into her reverie to tell her. Perhaps this was it, the news Lord Stratford was back in England at last and intending to have an answer to his offer of marriage. Now it came to it she was not quite as sure that she wanted to say yes as she had tried to convince herself she should since Darius Yelverton rejected her.

'Good morning,' Fliss said to the uncomfortable-looking country girl clutching a folded sheet of paper as if she would rather be a few miles away. 'I am Miss Grantham,' she said.

'A young miss gave me this back in Worcester when the stage was almost ready to go. Made me promise to hand it to you myself she did, miss. Name of Miss Defford, she said, miss. All of a pother, she was, said her purse had been took.'

Fliss's heartbeat raced as she realised Juno Defford had to have run away from London and her grandmother to be travelling by accommodation coach before she was robbed and things got even worse for her. 'Thank you for bringing it to me, but when was this?' she asked urgently, wondering how she could get to her former pupil before something even more dreadful happened to her.

'When we was about to leave, miss,' the girl said as if Fliss was slow on the uptake.

'And you came straight here?' Fliss asked, thinking she could calculate for herself if she knew that—it must have taken at three or four hours for the stage to get from Worcester to Broadley and ten or twenty minutes to walk here from the inn, depending how fast the girl went and what got in the way. Poor Juno must be frantic by now and it would take Fliss a couple of hours to get to Worcester even if she could find a fast carriage that would be ready to set out immediately.

'Yes, miss,' the girl said, looking very wary indeed about getting herself involved in any more of the young miss's tangles when she had done her a favour already by bringing the letter.

'Thank you, then… Oh, I am sorry, I do not know your name?'

'Mattie, miss. Mattie Carter.'

'Thank you for your kindness, then, Mattie, and the letter?'

'Here, miss.'

Fliss took it and grabbed a coin from the little bowl Miss Donne kept on the hall table for little everyday expenses. 'For your trouble,' she explained absently.

'Thank you, miss,' the girl said and went on her way.

Juno's handwriting on the rough paper made Fliss snap the makeshift seal in her hurry to read the hasty scrawl.

I had to run away, Miss Grantham. I have been robbed on the way to Worcester on the stage and will have to walk now. But it is summer and they say it is only twenty miles.

Please do not scold me when I get there. I

cannot marry Sir Gaulford Winkelowe and I
knew you would understand even if nobody
else can.

Would she? Fliss searched her memory for the
man and recalled Juno telling her the son of one
of her grandmother's oldest friends, who was old
enough to be her father, was always trying to squeeze
and kiss her if he managed to catch her alone. Surely
the Dowager would not force her granddaughter into
an April-and-December match simply to get the girl
off her hands?

Given her former employer's inability to admit
she was wrong and her always cavalier attitude to
her timid granddaughter, Fliss had the feeling the
Dowager could easily see it as the perfect solution
to an annoying problem. She should have tried much
harder to make Lord Stratford listen to her worries
for his ward and niece when she had the chance, Fliss
decided. It was her fault Juno was now wandering
around the country on her own, but never mind that
now. She must run round to Mrs Corham's since Miss
Donne was already there and three heads were better
than one so they could plan the search between them.

'The deuce! Where are you off to in such a tearing hurry?' Mr Yelverton demanded as he staggered
and held Fliss steady after the impact of her headlong body running smack into his.

'Please, you must let me go,' Fliss gasped and

tried to get her breath back. It felt as if she had run into a brick wall.

'Not when you are obviously in great distress,' he said with a formidable frown as he looked down at her bare headed and only lightly shod on such a threatening sort of morning.

'Yes, what on earth is so urgent you have to run, Fliss?' Marianne asked—Fliss had not even noticed her friend standing at her brother's side.

'I must find Miss Donne,' Fliss murmured and tried to dodge around Darius.

'No,' he said as if he had the right. 'Tell us what is wrong,' he demanded.

'Not here,' she answered and batted his hands away and sighed with relief when he let them drop and she was free again.

'Very well, we will follow you then,' he said and, as she did not want to waste any more time standing and arguing with him, she set off with both of them following behind as she led the way.

'Ah, we are off to Mrs Corham's house then,' Marianne murmured as they sped across the square and Fliss did not even have time to feel conscious that last time they were all here Darius had kissed her breathless, then walked away.

'I need to see Mrs Corham, Putkin,' she told the lady's butler breathlessly.

'Now, man,' Darius ordered the man in his best Captain Yelverton bark and the manservant stood aside as if his feet had moved before the rest of him had time to think about it, so Fliss was glad Darius and Marianne were here after all.

'Whatever is the matter, my dear?' Mrs Corham exclaimed as soon as she came out of the drawing room to see what the fuss was about and Fliss was already dashing towards her.

'It's Juno,' Fliss gasped out to Miss Donne, who would understand whom she meant without an explanation.

'Oh, my dear, but whatever has happened? You must come on in, all of you,' Miss Donne said and beckoned them inside, as if it mattered to Fliss who heard her.

'She has run away and must have had her purse snatched somewhere between London and Worcester, so she could not pay her fare for the rest of the way.'

'Where is she now?' Darius demanded. She had told him about her worries for her former pupil, had she not? At least he had grasped the magnitude of the problem even sooner than Miss Donne.

'She wrote that she will walk from Worcester to Broadley,' Fliss said and could not help wringing her hands like a stage heroine.

'That must be twenty miles and it looks as if it could pour with rain at any moment,' Marianne said as if even she would quail at such a walk and she must be the most intrepid female Fliss had ever come across.

'She must have set out hours ago now, since the

coach had to get here and the girl who brought it probably didn't hurry herself unduly on the way to find me and give me Juno's note. She could be anywhere along the way if she really has walked and who knows where she will find shelter if it does rain as heavily as it looks as if it might?' Now Fliss had given up hand wringing and taken up agitated pacing instead.

'Stop it,' Darius ordered her and he stepped forward so she had to stop, then he took her hands in his large ones and never had she needed such strength and certainty more. 'It will not help your friend one iota if you work yourself up into hysterics and are prostrated for the rest of the day when she needs you to be calm and thinking like a rational human being.'

'Well, really, Darius, that seems rather harsh,' his sister protested.

'No, he is quite right, Marianne, I was acting like a widgeon. Thank you,' she said and felt as if he had given her some sense back, despite the panic that was still threatening to paint her terrible pictures of her former pupil waylaid by villains or struggling on alone through a tempest. 'I came to ask for your help in organising a search for her, Mrs Corham. You know best who can be trusted with a young girl's safety and who might take advantage of her.'

'We could not hope to keep her escapade quiet,' the lady cautioned.

'As long as she is safe and dry I don't care about the rest,' Fliss said and it was quite true—if Juno was with her again and in one piece they could worry about the gossip later. Being safe and well was far more important than what people might say.

'It's all flummery beside her safety,' Darius agreed impatiently.

'So where should we start?' she asked Mrs Corham and the sooner they got on with it the better.

'I doubt anyone not used to hard walking could do it in much less than a day. She will have to stay on the road as she does not know the area and it does twist around the hills a good deal, but even so some of it is uphill.'

'Even so with such a start on us she could be more than halfway here by now,' Darius said and was obviously counting distances and calculating the time it would take him to get that far or maybe all the way to Worcester. 'If we hire a fresh horse for the gig, Marianne could drive that way and my Nero will be fresh enough to go cross country.'

'Putkin's nephews and sons-in-law will turn out to look for a vulnerable girl likely to get lost and soaked to the skin if we do not find her very soon. They are good boys and honest to a man, so you can trust them and Mr Yelverton to comb the roads between here and Worcester for her if they have to.'

'Can they ride?'

'Of course, that is why I suggested them.'

'Very well then, we must away to the George and hire every available horse in their stables.'

'My carriage horses can be ridden so that is two

more,' Mrs Corham said. 'A single horse can go where a carriage cannot and Putkin's boys know the hills far better than you do, Mr Yelverton, so I suggest they take the bridleways over the hills and you and your sister search the main road.'

'Where shall I go?' Fliss asked urgently.

'You have to stay here,' Darius ordered her and she frowned fiercely and raised her chin at him in defiance.

'Don't be ridiculous, I am the only one Juno knows, she needs me.'

'Exactly, that is why you have to be the one who stays here to welcome her back and let her know she truly is safe at last. She is going to need you here at the end of her long and weary journey,' Darius told her as if she was being a simpleton and slowing him down as well, then he must have seen the half-controlled terror in her eyes because he smiled reassurance and comfort and something a bit more personal before he was brisk again. 'We must have a good description of her. Height, build, hair colour— anything that might distinguish her from any other young ladies tramping the roads on such an unpromising day,' he added as if trying to lighten that terrible fear she was battling for her former pupil.

She managed to list every characteristic that made Juno her unique self and at least Miss Donne was collected enough by now to seize a pencil from her friend's secretaire and write it all down, then start copying it out for the various searchers to see.

'I suppose you are right,' Fliss said to Darius once she had finished and felt as if there ought to be something else she could do but watch and worry. 'Juno needs to find me here waiting for her or she would not have sent that letter.'

'And so she will,' he said and astonished her by grasping both her hands and kissing them one by one before he pulled gently away and went to consult Putkin then march off to the inn to begin the search.

'I had best go as well, but do try not to worry yourself to flinders,' Marianne said with a reassuring kiss on the cheek for Fliss and a hasty wave for the two older ladies before she followed her brother out of the room.

'I will go and make sure your Captain's men are properly organised,' Mrs Corham said with a look for Fliss that made her blush and wish he really was her Captain and never mind money and all the rest of the reasons why he was not.

'Mr Yelverton was right, you really need to be here when the girl gets here, my love,' Miss Donne protested several hours later when there was still no sign of Juno and one or two of Putkin's sturdy relatives had already returned from the search soaked to the skin and without a sign of the lost girl between here and Worcester. 'You are the only one of us the poor girl knows and she will be wet to the skin if she is still out in this, but she must still be very wary of anyone who answers this door but you and might not even agree to come inside.'

'It is going to pour even more furiously from the look of those black clouds and she could well be lost and alone out there somewhere while I stay here in the warm of your nice dry house. She will be terrified and soaked and could easily wander off the road and fall into a ditch; or she might lose her way; or be ambushed by some unscrupulous villain and carried off against her will. I simply must get out there and search for her as well, even I only wander around the approaches to the town to see her coming, so at least she will not be alone the rest of the way.'

'At least wait and see if the rest of the men or Mr Yelverton and Marianne found her on one of the roads and paths between here and Worcester. They might already have her with them and she will need comforting. Whatever adventures she has been on, she will only want to see you when she gets here since that is why she left home in the first place. You cannot fail her when she obviously trusts and loves you enough to flee to you when her life in London became unbearable.'

'I should have done more for her. You know as well as I do I could have gone to London to be with her and encouraged her throughout the ordeal of her debut. I have the means now and I did not use them to benefit her. It was so foolish of me to hide my good fortune from the world because I was unsure how

I felt about my choices and risk poor Juno's happiness and well-being.'

'I doubt Lady Stratford would have let you have much contact with her granddaughter even if you announced your good fortune and laid yourself open to real fortune hunters by joining them in London.' There was a question in Miss Donne's acute grey eyes that Fliss had been trying not to face since Darius kissed her hands and she began to question her aversion to that stormy emotion all over again. 'Is there no chance love might weigh more heavily in the balance than money for you than you thought, my dear?'

'Perhaps,' Fliss admitted gruffly. 'But how would I know once the news of my money got in the way? He wants to marry a fortune and I happen to have one.'

'Only you can answer that question, my dear, but make sure you do not lose what you need most while you are too busy looking for perfection to notice it.'

'When Mr Yelverton finds out I am an heiress and the granddaughter of an earl he will either be offended to his very soul that I did not tell him sooner or just as eager to marry my money as he would be any other heiress.'

'You spend too much time weighing up possibilities and not enough of it listening to your heart, Felicity. Apparently I taught you that much too well,' Miss Donne said sadly and shook her head.

'Never mind that now, I have to find Juno. If we

get to her soon enough, she might avoid an inflammation of the lungs and her young life is a lot more important than my tangled feelings.'

'No, maybe she is more urgent just at the moment but you are a good, kind girl who deserves more than you seem to expect from life.'

'Maybe I do and maybe I do not, but I still have to look for her, Miss Donne. I simply cannot stay here waiting to find out if the poor girl is safe or still lost one moment longer.'

'You might get lost yourself.'

'No, I can look after myself.'

'Then take my father's old boat cloak if you really must risk a soaking and come back the moment you find out if anyone has seen her.'

'Very well,' Fliss said with a look at the heavy clouds now beginning to hide the hills from view and her mind already on where to look first.

She had only meant to ask around to see if anyone had seen a girl walking alone towards the town, or if anything out of the ordinary had happened today that might give them a clue where Juno was. Now she was even more desperate to find Juno it did not seem very important who knew a young lady had run away from her family to find her former governess. Asking at the inns and posting house and venturing into the yards behind shops and warehouses to see if anyone could give her a clue to Juno's whereabouts had drawn a blank. She was near to giving up when

she spotted a narrow lane she had never noticed before. It seemed to slope up into the hills above the
town and turn into mere path and maybe everyone
else had forgotten such a minor way in and out of
the town.

'Where does the lane go?' she asked an old woman
sitting in the doorway of a windowless hovel smoking her pipe and watching the rain.

'Up over the common to Antsey.'

'Does it come out on the Worcester road?'

'Aye, in the end, but it would be a fierce way to go
and not much more than a sheep track for most of it.'

'But someone walking from that direction could
come down this way?'

'If they was daft or didn't want to be seen.'

'Thank you,' Fliss said and almost went back
down the road to ask if anyone had thought of searching this way. 'Has anyone passed this way lately?'
she asked.

'Ain't been anyone up or down here all day,' the
old woman said and shook her head at the very idea
anyone would want to go up there with such heavy
rain in the clouds that had been massing all day. 'No
place to get caught in bad weather, Antsey Hill,' she
warned, shook her head and shut the door behind her
as the rain began to fall more heavily.

Fliss had a sinking feeling that a sheep track over
the moorland would appeal to a girl who did not want
to be seen. Of course, Juno would have one eye on
the weather, even if she was desperate to get away

from the terrible situation she had been caught in by
her grandmother's ambitions, her uncle's absence
and Fliss's neglect. Or would she be so desperate
she forgot her usual common sense and battled on
through the storm? The more Fliss looked at the narrow path over the hills, the more she suspected Juno
would rather take it than risk being spotted trudging along the main road. If Fliss went back now she
would probably be told they would send someone up
this path in the morning and it was too treacherous to
search now. Juno might have been wet through and
lost on the hills all night by then and she would never
forgive herself if the girl took a fever after a night on
a rough common with little shelter for man or beast.

Chapter Fourteen

It had been raining hard for an hour now and instead of one lost girl they had two misguided and stubborn females to find. Darius bit back a curse and glared out of Miss Donne's cottage window at the heavy clouds and the misty blankness where the more distant hills used to be before they were lost behind a thick veil of rain. He should never have left Fliss here with nothing to do but fret. Thank God Miss Donne had had the sense to stay here and tell him what her former pupil had done. Marianne was disconsolately sipping hot chocolate by the fire and Miss Donne's maid had taken her soaking wet cloak off to be dried in front of the kitchen fire. At least that was two of the females he felt responsible for safely under one roof. He had best not let them know he felt that way or they would insist on going out in the pounding rain just to prove they were their own women.

'Where the devil can she have gone?' he demanded of the rain-streaked windowpane in sheer frustration.

'She could easily have given up and found shelter along the way by now. We will just have to trust in the girl's common sense now since nobody else could find her either,' his sister said, sounding weary and defeated.

'I meant Miss Grantham,' he said.

'So you did,' his sister said as if she ought to have known better.

'She should have stayed here. Now I have two of them to find.'

'A girl she loves is lost in the rain,' his sister excused Fliss with a shrug to say what else did he expect her to do? He was not quite sure that was any excuse for putting this sick dread in his heart that Fliss might have fallen and be lying unconscious in the rain taking her death of cold as they spoke. And to think he had ordered her not to panic when she found out her precious Juno was missing.

'I don't see what help she can be to anyone out in this,' he said. Then he heard a tap at the back door and was just in time to watch the maid warily open it against the onslaught of the rain and let a hunched figure slip inside before she slammed it behind him. Maybe one of the men was back with good news and he hoped none of them had got lost out on the roads around Broadley because he had enough on his plate right now. 'Who are you?' he barked as he barged into the kitchen as if he owned it.

'Name's Brown, your honour,' the bent little man

told him past a row of crooked and missing teeth that made Darius wish for an interpreter.

'Take you hat off when you speak to a gentleman,' the maid ordered. 'He's my granddad, sir,' she said as if that was a cross she had to bear.

'Oh,' Darius said, losing interest in a family visit on a wet day.

'My old lady said I had to come,' Brown said and the look on his face said how little he had wanted to in this weather. 'I told her they was out looking for a girl as had run away from London and she told me I had to come out in the rain and say what she saw because she wunt going to.'

'Sharp as a needle, our Gran,' the maid told Darius with a nod as if to say you can trust her say so even if Mr Brown is a fool.

'What did she see, then?'

Brown hesitated and Darius sighed slightly less loudly than the man's granddaughter when they both realised he wanted money.

'Tell the gentleman, or I'll let Gran know you didn't and she'll give you what for.'

'She says she spoke to a lady as the rain was starting to come down proper. Said it was a lady grown, though, and not a girl and she wanted to know where the lane went and had anyone else been up it today.'

'Where does it go?'

'Up over the hill to Antsey.'

'But it's no more than a sheep track and not a proper road at all, sir,' the maid answered Darius's next question before he could ask it. 'Only someone who knows it well or didn't want to be seen on the proper roads would risk it on such a day.'

Darius thought it sounded ideal for a girl who did not want to be caught and sent home with her tail between her legs by the local magistrate before she could even get to her destination and her former governess's fierce protection.

'Could a rider get up there?'

'Partway,' the old man said without much interest now he realised no reward was likely to come his way.

'And there's a bothy up there the shepherds use if they get caught on the hill by bad weather,' the maid added a lot more helpfully.

'Thank you. And please see that your grandmother gets this by way of a thank you,' he said and slipped a shilling into her hand.

'Aye, and don't give him a penny piece, sir, he'll only go to the nearest pub and waste it.'

But Darius was already on his way back to the cosy sitting room. 'Promise me you two will both stay here,' he demanded before he told either lady a thing. 'Swear it on a bible if you have one handy, Miss Donne; I cannot find time to rescue any more of you from your own folly in this weather, when it seems I already have my hands full of wrongheaded, reckless females today.'

'That really is very rude of you, Darius.'

'I feel rude. I now have to ride halfway up that confounded hill in the rain and rescue Miss Grantham from a foolish errand she ought never to have set out on in the first place. And I will have to drag some poor fool out with me so he can bring Nero home when I am forced to walk the rest of the way on a track no girl strange to the area could even find from the other end from the sound of it, let alone walking over it in the pouring rain. If only your precious friend Fliss would use her brains now and again instead of acting on impulse we would all be a lot happier and a great deal drier than I am about to be.'

'It will probably be dark by the time you catch up with her.'

'And thank you for that helpful observation, dear Sister.'

'Tie a blanket around your waist and take some food with you, Mr Yelverton.'

He could not refuse the plea in Miss Donne's eyes as she begged him to make her ewe lamb as comfortable as he could, if he actually managed to find her. 'There is a hut somewhere up there apparently,' he said to try to reassure her they would be safe when he did find her. And he would find her, he had to.

'Granddad said the hut is in the crook of the last bend from the top and there are three thorns in a row bent over like old women,' the maid told them as she hurried to fill a pack for him as best she could in such a hurry.

'Thank you for getting that out of him; that will make it much easier for me to find,' he said. 'Now, please will you two promise me you will stay here at least until morning?' he turned to demand of his sister and the lady of the house.

'I do,' Miss Donne said wearily. 'Just find my girl for me and keep her safe and dry tonight, Mr Yelverton.'

'Darius,' he argued and turned to stare at his sister until she sighed and agreed to stay here until morning. 'Thank you,' he said shortly and strode out into the pouring rain to find another idiot prepared to ride with him for however far his wet and already bad-tempered Nero would go and then bring him back again, hopefully without a good kicking for his trouble.

It took Darius over an hour to catch up with Miss Felicity Grantham even on horseback for half the way up the obscure track, then on foot once it got too narrow and he could bid goodbye to Nero and the bravest or most foolhardy of Putkin's various relatives. He was beginning to feel desperate as well as furious with her for persisting despite the tumbling rain. He was wondering if he had managed to miss her tracks when he finally saw her trudging determinedly up ahead in the early twilight and somehow the sight of her battling the wind and sheeting rain, but still doggedly going on, sparked his temper to new heights.

'What the devil do you think you are doing out in this, you damned fool woman?' he barked and felt even worse when she started at the sound of voice and nearly slipped on the sodden path.

'Being a damned fool woman in peace until you came along,' she told him stonily and kept walking doggedly on as soon as she had got her balance back.

'You have to stop,' Darius told her rather desperately, wondering how she was still managing to walk upright with so much water weighing down her cloak and all that mud on her boots. Probably everything else she had on underneath the cloak would be soaked with this endless, incessant rain by now as well. Instead of listening to him, she trudged on as if he had not spoken. This was probably not the right time to tell her that her bonnet was so limp and useless and bedraggled she might as well take it off and throw it away for all the protection it gave her raindarkened hair. 'Seriously, Fliss, you have to come back to Broadley before you die of exposure up here.'

'No,' she said with one glance up at him and a shake of her head that scattered heavy raindrops without making her look any less wet. If only he could spare attention from his footsteps and not slipping on this sodden slope he would like to shake her until she had to see sense. But, no, he denied the harsh impulse—no, he would not even if he had the balance for it. He pitied her and admired her far too much to do anything of the sort.

'Stop!' he shouted above the relentless beat of the rain. 'What good will it do Miss Defford if you are lost and soaking wet in these hills and have to be searched for as well? You are not immune to the ills of humanity simply because you love her.'

'What if she is out all night in this?' she almost had to shout back against the relentless beat of the rain and he was worried about the effort it cost her as he blinked against the force of that rain to peer down at her pale, exhausted-looking face. 'I will not stop looking for her as long as there is breath in my body,' she went on stubbornly and why was she so curst unreasonable?

'What use will you be when all you can do is join her in being lost and soaked through, you stubborn half-witted female?' he shouted over the rain and even the summer daylight was fading early on them now because of the heavy pall of cloud looming over them like the last judgement.

'Company,' she told him shortly.

'On your deathbed?' he argued again and this really had to stop now.

'What about you, Mr Yelverton? You have dependents, I do not.'

'Which makes it perfectly all right for you to risk your life in a wrong-headed quest to find your former pupil when half the men in the district are out looking for her and a lot more familiar with it than you are, does it? What if they have already found her and now have to turn out again on such a night to find you instead? What could you be doing to those good men and their families by continuing against all the odds and courting an inflammation of the lungs?'

'She is so young and so alone,' she replied as if it was a sort of agony for her to think of her former pupil lost and lonely on such a night. He sensed guilt that she had not been able to fight harder for the girl when her grandmother insisted on carrying her off to London and making her face crowds of people that terrified her. That guilt belonged on the old lady's shoulders instead of his Fliss's. When had he begun to call her his Fliss in the privacy of his own head? As soon as Marianne let her nickname slip, he supposed, and finally let himself know how precious this mulish and wrong-headed female was to him, now it felt as if it was almost too late to tell her so.

'If you have managed to teach her anything at all, she will have too much sense to risk herself in such a storm. She will have taken shelter as soon as the rain came on so hard and she is no doubt huddled in front of some kind soul's fire, drinking soup and listening to the rattle of this downpour on their windows and thanking God she is inside and not out in it like we are.'

He let the shiver he had been fighting for her sake shake him visibly as rain poured down his neck and even his sturdy beaver hat could not keep him dry any longer. He saw her expression turn from set determination to doubtful and concerned. Of course, that was the secret with her, wasn't it? Appeal to her worry about everyone around her instead of trying to make her see sense about herself. 'My shoulder aches like the devil,' he murmured as if the rather minor

pain of it had ground those words out of him. He hid
a wry smile as she looked anxiously around them
for some sort of shelter to save a not very wounded
soldier from taking an ague. Now he had to hide a
pang of guilt when a frown of concern knitted her
finely marked chestnut brows, as if she was furious
with herself for not protecting him now instead of her
pupil. She would be a trial to be so close to for the
rest of his life, he decided, as the truth of their position sank in and he found he did not hate the thought
of that joint future one little bit. It felt as if that was
what had been meant to be all along, if only he had
listened to his heart and instincts and recognised her
as his fate a lot sooner.

They had to find that shepherd's hut now though
and he thought it could only be a few hundred yards
away in the next hollow of thorn-sheltered bushes,
since they were so near the top and they would have
to stay there for the night now there was no sign
of this downpour stopping. If they both survived
this soaking, they would have to marry after that.
Good—well, that was the rest of his life settled then.
His inner Darius gave a sigh of relief and a catlike
stretch of satisfaction because now he had no choice.
He could do what he had wanted to from the instant
he laid eyes on Miss Felicity Grantham in that wood
in all her muddy glory, he could marry her and forget
all about fortune hunting. They would find a way to
manage on hard work and love somehow or another.

'I can hardly see a thing,' he heard her confess

and felt his heart turn over as he gazed down at her through the pouring rain and the brooding dusk.

'I think we must be near to a shepherd's bothy I was told about. We will have to hope they saw this downpour coming and got their sheep down from the hills in time or it might already be full of shepherds.'

'I don't care,' she said, as if his pretend-weakness had let out the desperation she had probably been feeling all the way up this hill.

'Come on, then,' he said as encouragingly as he could manage and wound an arm about her narrow waist to help her through the sodden undergrowth and over the crest of this last small hill and down again. Yes, he was right. Thank God, the three thorn trees loomed over them and there was the squat little hut, built into the side of the hill and meant to withstand this sort of foul weather and even deep snow if it came too early or late to be predictable on this marginal land.

There was no smoke from the chimney, he finally managed to see past the raindrops caught up in his eyelashes. He blinked them away and watched their footsteps carefully in the gloom. It would be cold and probably damp inside it without a fire, but at least Fliss would not have to be miserably self-conscious and cling to her soaked garments without a lot of dour strangers looking on while she tried to get warm. Any red-blooded male would be all too ready to sneak a sly look if she had to strip her wet clothes off in company and she would have to do so if she was to avoid a chill and he doubted the blanket would be as dry as he would like by now even under his coat. 'Nearly there,' he added as he felt her mould herself even closer to his body as if she was nearly spent.

He hesitated on the edge of calling her his love in the privacy of his own head, but even with her pressed up against him and shivering he could not quite let that last ounce of stubbornness go just yet. She was his touchstone for all other women, he realised that now he had the truth of her in his arms and his head. She was his passion and maybe his delight when she realised the truth as well, but love cost too much. Loss was the flip side of love, the abyss on the other side that made it too much of a risk for rational human beings. He still was not quite prepared to lose his very self in his wife, or encourage her to do the same, but he knew he already cared for Fliss far more than he had intended to care for a wife. There was already a giant crack running through his resolution to protect the woman he married from crushing loss by not letting her love him in the first place.

'I am all right; I can stand on my own,' she murmured when he stopped in front of the heavy oak door now dark with rain instead of the usual silvery grey after years of keeping out the cold and wet. He cast her a doubtful look and wondered if he could lift the heavy baulk of wood across the door one-handed, but that would give the lie to his story even if he thought he did have the strength for it and they might both fall over if he failed.

'Best get it done, then,' he said gruffly and it felt like the hardest thing he had ever had to do as he left her to wobble on weary legs and soaking wet feet so he could grasp the beam with both hands. 'Here we are then, at last. Best take off your muddy shoes if you are not going to ruin the carpets, my lady. I hear that the maids in these parts get very cross if you track mud across their nice clean floors.'

'I heard it was their year off,' she managed to joke weakly. How many women would find any humour at all in their position, although Darius supposed she was probably too weary and spent to realise the full implications of the night they were about to spend together?

'Let us hope so,' he murmured as he pushed the heavy door to behind them and thanked whoever had built this strong refuge for a small glazed window. 'There will be a flint somewhere and dry kindling,' he said as much to reassure himself as her. It was summer and it might not have felt urgent to replace the stores used up on fickle spring nights until late autumn.

'Is this rain ever going to stop?' she said as if he ought to know.

'Unless this is the end of days, yes, and since I do not think this place would float we must hope for sooner rather than later.'

'I doubt if two of every creature on earth would

fit into such a small space even if we were inclined to share it with them for forty days and forty nights like Noah and his long-suffering family.'

'I always used to wonder why they did not eat one another and what on earth everyone ate for all that time.'

'Yes, indeed. The Ark must have been vast.'

'We could do with a couple of big shaggy dogs for you to cuddle up and get warm while I struggle to get a fire going,' he tried to joke, but the dimness inside the hut was making it hard to find the makings of one that he hoped had been left here.

'Since they would be soaking wet and muddy as well as us if we had any with us, I vote for a good fire instead,' she said and seemed to revive as she crossed to the closed door to let the fading light in as well as a smattering of rain.

'Thank you, and I am sorry I shouted at you,' he said, the absurdness of polite conversation striking him as he finally found the box of dry kindling and moss and set about building a fire from twigs and thanked God for the dry logs waiting to go on it when it was hot enough. All he needed now was a flame. 'Best shut the door now I have what we need, the sparks will be blown out by that dratted wind otherwise.'

'Very well, Captain,' she said and shut it smartly. 'Anything else?'

She was a strong woman, wasn't she? Many women

would slump in a corner and count their ills in her shoes, aye, and most of the men as well.

'Not now,' he said gruffly as he bent over the flints and struck them clumsily together until he got his hand in and a more promising spark flared in the semi-darkness. Best not think about the ridiculous reply that sprang into his mind at her meant-to-be joking question.

Yes, come and wrap yourself around me until we are both so warm we need not worry about a fire at all.

But he was meant to be a gentleman, wasn't he?

'There, I think it will take this time,' he said instead as he blew gently on the smouldering moss and held it close to the wood shavings and twigs on the rough hearth.

'Oh, well done,' she said as flame flared and he set it to climb into the budding fire and felt as if he had completed a labour of Hercules.

Best not look at her until he had calmed down again, he decided as he sat back on his heels to watch the infant fire as if it fascinated him. At last it was hot enough to add a couple of skinny logs and turn away. He might be cool enough now not to bother her with a masculine obsession even she would soon pick up despite her governessly innocence, so he had best not think about his fantasy of her curled into his lap as they watched the flames together as lovers.

'Miss Donne and the maid insisted on putting food in my pack, although goodness knows what it is when we were all in such a hurry,' he said although he was not hungry, or at least not for food.

'And there will be plenty of water if we put that pot outside under the eaves,' she said as if she was thinking about getting wet again.

'I will do that; you get closer to the fire.'

'You are just as wet as I am and it is my fault you had to come out looking for me because I wanted to find poor little Juno so badly.'

'Poor little Juno risks feeling the flat of my hand on her backside if you take a chill after all that walking in the rain for no reason. She could have written to her guardian or found a more rational way to escape her grandmother's plans rather than striding into strange countryside on the verge of the worst storm even the locals have seen in years.'

'Better than being forced into marriage with a man she hardly knows.'

'So you would have done the same in her shoes?'

'I don't know, I have never been in such a situation.'

Well, you are now, he argued silently, but if she was too dazed and cold and worried to think that out for herself yet all well and good.

'There, that's water dealt with and, before you ask, yes, I rinsed it out and, no, I did not drown any spiders.'

'I wasn't going to ask that.'

'No? My sister would have done.'

'She must have had to make far worse places than

this a home for the time being when she was in Spain and Portugal.'

'Yes, and I suppose she was right to insist on following the drum when she married Daniel Turner.'

'Of course she was. Think how little time she and her husband would have had together if she had stayed in England or Lisbon instead.'

'Aye, she loved him,' he said, staring down into the fire as if it might conjure an image of his dead friend and brother-in-law. 'I thought she would break when he was killed,' he confessed to the glowing flames and shivered at the memory of Marianne so stricken and nothing he could do or say was any help.

'She is stronger than that.'

'But why should she have to be? Why love as she loved with such a fearsome risk at the end of it?'

'Because if a person refuses to let love in they will be lonely for the rest of their days and regret it for ever.'

'Yet I never saw anything lonelier than my sister longing for her Daniel every moment and hour of the day after he was killed. It seemed as if all the life had seeped out of her and she was little more than a walking ghost of herself. I would never want to leave behind that sort of sorrow for a woman I loved.'

'What right would you have to make her choices for her?' she challenged as if this had suddenly become a very personal conversation and it could not be.

'None at all, but if I refuse to love her in the first

place it will save her a deal of worry and aggravation, don't you think?' he asked half-seriously.

'No, I think you deserve both in spades for thinking you can order your emotions like a company of soldiers and ignore a woman foolish enough to want to love you anyway.'

'Why on earth would she? I have seen things I really hope you never even have to dream about in your worst nightmares, Miss Grantham. I have done things that turn my stomach just thinking about. I am not a fit man to lay down his heart and soul for his lover to pick up if she chooses to blight her life with my wrong deeds and omissions. Somewhere along the way to Toulouse and peace I lost the Darius Yelverton who grew up in Bauxhall village with two mischievous little sisters. *His* worst sins were staying out later than he should with his friends once or twice and refusing to learn his lessons as well as he could have done with a little more application. Oh, and he once hung Cook's best flannel petticoat from the church tower because one of those friends of his bet him half a crown he would not and he could never resist a dare.'

'That boy is not as far away from you as you seem to think. I catch glimpses of him now and again and please don't think that piece of devilment has shocked me because I would have joined in with it given half a chance if only I had known you then. I very much doubt that side of you is dead at all, Mr Yelverton. Perhaps you simply need to rediscover the

light-hearted boy you hid away when you took on
Captain Yelverton's command and all that responsibility for other people's lives.'

'And perhaps I need to talk less and do more,' he
said uneasily as he looked about this spartan little
room for something more to be doing. There was a
smoke-blackened pot that must have been used for
cooking and a roughly made cup to drink out of and
not much else. 'Thank goodness it is summer and
we are hardly likely to freeze to death before we are
found come morning,' he said gloomily.

'Don't,' she said with a mighty shiver as if even
the thought of it was making her feel colder and wet-
ter and what could he do about it?

'I will go and get some more wood in before the
light goes completely,' he said to get himself out
of here without suggesting they took all their wet
clothes off and clung together to share warmth. It
would be sensible and practical, but was sure to lead
to consequences she was certainly not ready for after
her gruelling climb up this hill in the teeth of common sense and self-preservation.

Chapter Fifteen

Fliss thought he was embarrassed by their situation and wishing he could get away from her. Or maybe he could read her mind and see the shameful thoughts she was battling with. She had been so pleased to see him when he stormed up behind her and shouted over the downpour at her. She had to bite back a plea to simply hold her close and steam gently with her in the rain.

Except there was nothing gentle about it and now the rain was teeming relentlessly down outside the sturdy walls of this shelter as if determined they would not escape a night in this warming and sparse little room in the middle of nowhere.

Well, she was in perfect harmony with the rain for once today then; she did not want it to suddenly stop and the moon to come out so they could walk downhill with all that weight of water in their clothes and only a mile or so to go before they were safe and respectable.

She shifted under her sodden cloak and wondered about the wisdom of taking it off. Best not to know what she looked like, but she put up a hand to her ruined bonnet and decided that could go for all the use it was now. As far as she was concerned it could go on the fire, except it would probably put it out in its sodden state. She had never liked it and undid the rain-hardened bow with difficulty, then flung it aside to dry and perhaps be fed to the fire later when it was not quite as wet.

She shifted her wet shoulders under the weight of the cloak Miss Donne had made her wear and thanked her mentor for doing so even as she felt oppressed by the weight and wetness of it until she decided she was better off without that as well. There, that was better. She moved closer to the hearth and wondered about letting down her sodden hair to dry in front of the now-blazing fire.

Why not? It was not as if Darius had never seen her wet and unkempt before and with her hair all over the place. At least this time she was relatively clean. She refused to look at her petticoats and find out that was a lie, but she was certainly a lot cleaner than she had been the first time they met so that would have to do.

Do for what, Felicity? For the reckless plan she had in mind since she realised he was too much of a gentleman to plot her downfall. She would have to do it herself as he was such a gallant idiot he probably thought she had no idea they were already hopelessly compromised. After a night alone in this remote hut they would have very little choice but to marry or be scandalous and all her uncertainty had melted away now they were inevitable.

Of course he had no idea she had inherited the fortune he wanted so badly and she squirmed in her wet cotton skirts as she wondered how he would react when he knew the secrets she had been keeping from him. She supposed she ought to tell him before they did anything irrevocable. Yes, she definitely ought to say something about the money, but why had he ever thought money was important in the first place? Apparently she was still too angry with him to mention it now and how was that supposed to go anyway?

Oh, by the way, Mr Yelverton, I have a personal fortune of thirty thousand pounds I think you might find quite useful when you have to marry me, once we have spent the night here and made love, as we are definitely going to do as soon as we are drier and a bit warmer and I can remind you how hotly and sweetly we kissed one another in the shadowy warmth of Mrs Corham's rose garden.

Honesty was a virtue, but not one she was willing to embrace at the cost of sitting in a cold corner of this bare little room opposite to his cold corner of it all night long, while she brooded about Juno and her possible fate in a strange country in the pouring rain and he brooded about her failure to tell him he could marry her and have the fortune he wanted so badly right from the start.

'I need him too much,' she whispered to the fire and even had to back away from it a little when the fierceness of its heat stung her face and proper Miss Grantham added that to an all over blush at Fliss's scandalous intentions. Now she could actually see her clothes steaming and felt her heavy hair at least stop dripping raindrops so it did not feel quite as much like rats' tails. 'Not a very attractive picture, Felicity,' she told herself wryly as she combed her fingers through her still-wet hair and wondered how many logs Darius was thinking of fetching in while he was out there in the near dark, trying not to think about him making love to her.

He came in at long last, shouldering the heavy door open. She remembered his injury as he hefted a great armful of logs into the stone box someone had built at the side of the fire, presumably to keep them dry enough to burn without risk of setting light to the lot and smoking the weary shepherd back out into the cold. But what damage had Darius done to himself riding in the rain for hours, then slipping and sliding through the mud chasing after her?

'There's a privy close to the log store,' he told her gruffly. 'Best put my coat on over your cloak now you are beginning to dry out a little.' He shrugged the heavy wetness of it off before she could argue and it was considerate of him to think of the mun-

dane details of life while she was sitting here plotting his downfall.

With a sigh she rediscovered her ex-bonnet and
plonked it back on her head, then added his coat as
ordered and marched outside in the last threads of
daylight to do as she was bid. It was a relief and so
good to be able to put off all those layers as soon as
she scurried back into the bothy and the warmth of it
felt delightful now the fire was reaching every cold
corner. And handsome, about-to-be-seduced Darius
Yelverton was waiting for her with a cautious smile
of welcome and something a great deal hotter in his
light blue eyes he obviously hoped she did not know
about, the great gallant fool. He carefully draped
their outer clothing from hooks that must have been
put in for the purpose, as if that might fend off the
hopes and dreams he was about to have with her
whether he liked it or not. Fliss supposed even poor
commoners must have a change of clothes to wear
turn and turn about when they lived in this ridiculous climate and needed to hang drying clothes or
perhaps their food up away from vermin. And now
Fliss really had endured enough of him avoiding the
subject uppermost in both their minds so it was high
time he stopped avoiding her gaze and paid attention
to her instead of the little domestic details of their
life up here in the wilds.

'We need to share warmth,' she informed him
boldly. He looked as if she had struck him with a
stout club, so she floundered around for a good rea-

son why, since he did not look as if he liked the idea much. 'You have an injury you might have disturbed after a day searching in the rain and I refuse to let it turn into a permanent weakness for lack of a little warmth. I refuse to have you on my conscience as well as Juno.'

'My arm is perfectly fine and we are hardly in the Pyrenees in mid-winter,' he said as if that made all the difference and how could he be so rational and obtuse?

'Maybe it would be better if we were,' she replied impatiently.

'No,' he said with an emphatic shake of the head. 'We would starve to death up here or freeze trying to get down to the nearest village.'

'Then I am very thankful we are only in Herefordshire in the pouring rain,' she said with what she thought was exemplary patience.

'And it is quite warm in here now,' he added as if that was a good thing.

'Oh, dear, so it is. Well then, we had better just sit and stare at the fire from opposite corners of the room and say nothing more to one another until it is daylight again and we can go home.'

'That is not what I meant.'

'Is it not? You did not mean to stand as far away from me as possible like an outraged dowager, then? And you need to work on your society manners before you go looking for a rich wife again, Mr Yelverton.'

'We both know I will not be doing that,' he said gruffly.

'Do we?' she said rather wilfully, then decided to let him off the hook when he looked sheepish and self-conscious and a little bit annoyed. 'Yes, I know you will have to marry me and I must marry you after tonight, whether we spend it as stiff and cold as a pair of bodkins and as far apart as the North and South Poles, or lying in one another's arms like a pair of turtledoves.'

'True,' he said as if holding back a sigh by the skin of his teeth.

'A lady does like to feel at least a little bit welcome in her future husband's bed,' she said huffily and decided to turn her back on the fire and him to dry her tangled hair properly after all, since she was obviously not going to be spending a night in his powerful arms and she didn't want him to see how disappointed she was.

'You have no idea what you are provoking,' he warned her.

She shot him a sidelong look and why was he still standing by the fire like a pillar of stern respectability when she had nerved herself to take the initiative and he had not taken her up on her outrageous offer? Had he no idea how much it cost a former governess to abandon all her upright habits and encourage a gentleman to seduce her in the firelight? 'Then show me,' she said with a shrug designed to provoke him a lot more.

'Have you any idea how little that gown leaves to my imagination now you are soaking wet again?' he said as if she might have turned into a wilful seductress while they were not looking and planned a runaway girl, this summer tempest and the now-cosy little bothy where they could be marooned together all so she could have her evil way with him. 'Have you any idea how little the muddy one you had on the first day we ever met showed me? You managed to torture me with frustrated desire for the lush body underneath it all the way from Brock Wood back to Owlet Manor and I wanted you painfully and urgently then, just as I want you even more desperately right now, Miss Felicity Grantham, so kindly stop playing with fire and behave yourself.'

'It was not my fault I was wet and muddy then, but I must admit being almost as wet if a lot less muddy today was entirely my own doing.'

'And I admit it was by accident you drove me to the edge of madness back then, but right now it feels as if you are torturing me on purpose. You have no idea what you are asking for, do you, Miss Felicity Grantham?'

'Now I think that I have at the very least a shrewd notion what we are both longing to do to each other under all your gallant arguments, Mr Darius Yelverton. But I also think I have had enough of lowering myself to ask for it, so I will bid you a goodnight. Perhaps you can work out how we are to be found miles away from one another and having slept in separate shelters for the night by tomorrow morning so we can preserve your pristine reputation as a gentleman for you and you need not wed such a brazen hussy after all.'

'No chance of that,' he murmured as if the words were racked out of him. 'I am not leaving you alone here and I wish you would stop calling my future wife names,' he said softly and held out his hands for hers with a silent demand she answered a bit too willingly.

She ought to make him beg after such a cross and clumsy wooing, but the awful truth was she wanted him too much to wait for the right words. She gave a funny little gasp of shock and satisfaction as he tugged her to her feet as if he had lost all his gentlemanly restraint in one go, then she was hard up against his rampantly aroused body as if that was what they had been made for and he kissed her as if his next breath depended on it. His mouth was fierce on hers, his body so rigidly aroused against hers no wonder he had been trying to keep her at a distance, the great gallant idiot. He was hard, all over and where she had been fantasising he would be again for her ever since that sinful night under the stars when he kissed her as if she was vital to his health and continuing sanity. And here were his magical, provoking hands on her again as she had so often dreamt they could be ever since they aroused her to such a pitch of wanting and needing the last time. His palms and long, strong fingers were hard from the physical toil he undertook day after day on his home farm and she loved the work-hardened strength of them. She wriggled a little closer and shaped herself to his caress as she loved the fact he knew what a hard day's work meant. There was no softness or signs of too much wine and luxury and nothing much to do in her lover's touch, or anywhere else on his sleekly muscular body for that matter. 'Oh, yes, touch me some more,' she demanded as he seemed to try to draw back and remember to protect her from his masculine urges and rampant need. She leaned up into his mouth and kissed him, grabbing the reins impatiently from his too-gallant hands and feeling like a silken goddess ready to shoot fire from her fingertips if her passions were not stoked higher and harder very soon and he did not stop being such a confounded gentleman.

'My hands are rough,' he murmured as if he should apologise for them.

'I know,' she said on a delighted moan as the slightly abrasive hardness of them explored her body and caused so much havoc she loved every whisper of them down her suddenly sensitive backbone. They lingered at the narrowness of her waist for a moment and she quivered with impatience for more. No need to tell him she liked it when she was curving herself into his body like a wanton and a small voice in her head whispered she was shameless. She knew she had been secretly on fire for him ever since the night he first kissed her, but tonight she would have so much more to look forward to that she ached for it. This felt like the rightful continuation of that night when he insisted they leave off seducing one another when sanity intruded and he must have recalled she was supposed to be penniless.

No, don't think about that now, Felicity.

Where were they? Ah, yes, his magically roughened hands were asking for permission over the delicate skin of her buttocks and her damp gown and she could squirm into his touch with a delicious little shimmer of pleasure and forget he wanted to marry for money or start away from him like an outraged virgin. Since she wanted him to carry on seducing her as well it hardly seemed worth having too good a memory right now. She would go for the moment and let tomorrow take care of itself. So she shuffled even closer to his mighty, aroused body and heard him groan with need. The sound sparked a delicious feeling of triumph deep inside her that felt like a joint enterprise at last. He might not want to want a governess, but right now he really, really did. 'Does it feel as if I mind?' she asked through kiss-numbed lips and hardly recognised the sound of her own voice under all that husky encouragement.

'Mind what?' he said and kissed her again as if he was starving for her and had been ever since that magical night.

And didn't that make him a great, bumbling fool to risk all this for mere money? Chiding him for it in her head, she still could not get enough of him in the moment and stretched herself on tiptoe to meet his kiss closer and closer and every bit of her that could get close to him was wrapped into him as if they were kissing all over with their bodies, wanting one another all over. Desperate for one another all over, she discovered through the heat haze of her own desire as she felt him stiffen even further against her core and this wild heat shot lightning through her until her legs wobbled and she could no longer stand.

He felt them go, too, and swept her even closer in so he could take the weight off them altogether and she draped herself against him as if all the firmness had left her bones. They felt weightless, she decided fancifully and took a moment to doubt it as she loved the strength and might of him and felt a little bit guilty about wrapping herself around him like ivy. 'Where?' she murmured as if that was all the questions they needed about what came next. Maybe it was, because the fire inside her was threatening to burn her up as he sank on to his knees on to that precious blanket he managed to bring with him for her comfort and she followed his every move like a fiery, feminine force of nature.

He sat back on his heels and she knew he was protecting her as best he could, from the mightiness and depth of his passion as well as the hardpacked earth floor beneath them. He shifted a little further back and silenced her little mewl of protest with a kiss even as he found her laces and freed her from lawn and cambric so his hands could adore her breasts, even if he lacked patience enough to rid her of her corset as well and it only pushed them even more eagerly into his hands. He murmured something wondering and praising, as if he had truly been longing to shape and arouse and explore them from the moment they met as he claimed he had just now. Her nipples felt hot and desperate for his touch and he insisted on letting his wickedly knowing touch whisper all around them first. She felt them tighten almost to the point of pain before he flicked a long finger across the tip of one and shot fire straight to her feminine core and made her keen with hunger.

A huge frustration built ever higher inside her just as his driven kiss on her driven kiss back drove it hotter and ever more demanding. He was a magician who could rouse every inch of her all at the same time. She bent even closer into his wickedly arousing mouth as his tongue plunged into hers with a rhythm her body wanted to take up and run with while his wicked fingers were busy with the laces of her gown. She heard herself go breathless with hot yearning and desperate anticipation that there must be yet more glory on its way for both of them. She writhed against him in search of that beat he had set their tongues again and he soothed her urgent mouth with gentler kisses. She gasped out first a protest, then praise as his mouth abandoned hers to play with her edgily roused nipples.

His wickedly arousing tongue licked and teased her to the edge of reason—the wet tightness of her skin remembered the richness of a banquet even when he moved on, looking serious and utterly absorbed in her when she stared up at him to find out what was happening now. Then his wonderful hands were on her bare ankle as he caught the hem of her gown and she shifted all too willingly as he swept it out from under her and let it pool about her knees. When had he padded that dirt floor with his jacket as well as the roughness of that blanket, to save her from as much discomfort as he could? He was a considerate lover and a fine man, despite all his claims to the contrary. He spared her a hot smile and a wry twist of one eyebrow as if to say *are you still ready for this?*

She frowned impatiently back at him to say, *of course*, and could not help a heavy-eyed, slightly sidelong glance and a seductress's smile. He smoothed a wickedly encouraging finger up her outer thigh and did nothing to force the pace or storm through to the fury of need and excitement she could almost feel coming off him in waves of sensual heat. She closed her eyes briefly, then opened them to let him see how much she wanted this, how desperately she ached for him at the feminine heart of her. She had not even known that it could be as harshly, beautifully, aroused as it was right now until the ache was a hot and physical pain as well as a deep and joyous anticipation.

'I ache for you—ah, Darius, I want you,' she told him incoherently. 'So much,' she added on a sigh as she leant towards him and pushed recklessly against the very emphatic evidence that he wanted her back.

'Careful,' he cautioned her, as if that was even possible now they had got this far. 'I want you too much,' he added on a sigh that made her heart melt with some last level of heat and wanting he had not let them know about until now.

'Never,' she promised him huskily. 'You will never be too much for me, Darius,' she added and stared at him solemn-eyed. That was all the promises he would let her make, she knew it and accepted it would have to be enough, for now. 'How could you be when I need you so desperately I feel like fire?'

He looked driven and intent and desperate back and she dared hope he felt something unique for her as well. He worked that wicked, knowing hand of his to the privacy between her legs and even managed to shoot her a hot look, then a boyish shrug, as she forced her attention away from fascination with his fire-shadowed face to what they were going to be doing to one another very shortly now. He looked magnificent in the glow of firelight that seemed to linger lovingly on the sharp planes of his high cheekbones and the manly vulnerability of his firm mouth as he concentrated on showing her pleasure before he even thought about his own. She was almost so caught up in the delight of being able to watch him openly and without secrets, or not many of them anyway, that she let the novel heat he was stoking in a place she hardly even knew she had until tonight share space with that less earthy pleasure. Soon his touch there was so emphatic she stared at him wide-eyed and felt colour and hot excitement flame her cheeks and threaten to take her over altogether. She shook her head as something huge and wonderful, but a little bit lonely, threatened to overwhelm her. 'With you,' she demanded incoherently. 'Only with you,' she added with a challenge in her gaze to let him know it was a condition for the next leap over this precipice he was holding her over as if he still wanted to tip her over it alone.

'There will be no going back, then,' he cautioned her as if he thought she might just get up and plump for that night of staring into the fire alone after all.

'Idiot,' she said and shook her head at him to make him see how impossible it was for her.

'And it will hurt,' he added with such concern in his eyes she was afraid he might still baulk and re-fuse to carry on making love to her to the nth degree of bliss as her now-frantic need whispered he could.

'Always?'

'No, just the once,' he promised so sincerely she felt tears threaten as she bent closer to meet his gaze as close as they could get without going out of focus.

'Then I want that pain in order to get to the other side of it with you, Darius,' she told him so earnestly he smiled and her knees went boneless again, so it was just as well he was taking the weight off them and finally lifting her even closer, astride his bent-up knees and against his striving, rigidly aroused manhood, but not quite over it yet. She heard him take in a great sigh of breath as if he had to do it to gentle himself enough for her and his hand drove her a little further up that lovely slope of wanting and needing until she could almost sense the wonder on the other side of it and squirmed in protest yet again.

'Lean upwards a little,' he urged her with unsteadily murmured words and his urgent touch on her narrow back and down to cup her softly curved bottom. 'That's it, lover,' he whispered and now the core of her was resting on the very tip of him and she felt alive as she never had in her life before. He was so gentle with her, so careful to ease her striving, hot sex on to his she fought her own impatience to let him be the man she loved more deeply with every breath she took.

'I won't break,' she told him in a burst of edgy eagerness and felt his sex bump up against the barrier he was so intent on getting her over as lightly as possible.

'I might,' he told her with an almost-laugh, all his attention centred on them joined as they were by whatever this was, yet something intense and sweet in his eyes as they met hers said it would be worth it for the rest of their lives.

'Do it now, please, Darius? Or I might have to,' she urged him as she felt the novelty of tightening on him inside her and his sex kicked and seemed to go even harder as if it needed all his iron willpower to control it after that wilful provocation.

So he did and he was right. It did hurt. For a stinging moment she had to fight an instinct to jump up,
break this intimacy and have him out of her body
once and for all. He knew it; he felt her fight herself and looked ready to let her go, but she shook
her head and remembered the urgency and delight
of only moments ago and decided to trust it instead
of the discomfort and strangeness of him inside her.
'Make it feel good again, Darius?' she pleaded and
he smiled that wry, intimate smile of his and found
the knot of pleasure at her core again unerringly
and somehow, between his incendiary touch and the
heady novelty of having his mightily aroused sex so
deep inside her, she began to forget the fleeting pain
of losing her maidenhood and re-entered their fiery
race for the great finish line she had sensed before.
Only now it felt like so much more of a prize with
him galloping headlong for it as well.

'Oh, that feels so good, so right,' she gasped out
as he thrust up into her ever faster and more desperately and surely they would break if they did not
get there soon? His all was centred on her all and
the thrust and parry was such a sweet novelty she
writhed and shuddered with the absolute pleasure of
it hot and hungry inside her where she was joined
to him. Then they spun. That was the only word she
could reach for as they spun up and away and into
somewhere rich and strange and ruled by wave after
wave of exotic pleasure that shook her to the core and
with him so driven and pleasured inside it as well.

Bucking and bowing against the gentled strength of his mighty arms, she lost herself in him. They convulsed together on a great wave of sated pleasure and she would think they must be spent, then yet another shockwave would shoot through them like a wonder built exclusively for them, tailor made for their joint ecstasy. She heard their gasps and moans and shouts of absolute pleasure as words melted away from both of them. Until finally those intimate lovers' noises sank to contented sighs and little mews and moans of sheer delight, so she had to be glad they were miles away from any other human beings and had stood no chance of being overheard. This little world felt too exclusive and pleasurable and private for anyone else to know about.

They parted so reluctantly she ached for their physical intimacy, but he cuddled her against him instead, shuffling them over to the fire to put on more wood. When had he had the presence of mind to put her cloak in front of the fire to dry enough to cover her when they had done loving? For now. She found his poor mistreated coat in the shadows where they had left it, then insisted he used it to shield himself from the floor as they cuddled together in the firelight.

'I don't think I have had a female fuss over me so much since I fell out of the Sexton's cherry tree on to my head as a boy,' he teased her and it felt wonderful he could do that after they had just repainted the stars and she was glad he did not regret it either.

They both knew this meant they were together for life and she expected him to be disappointed about all the things he could not now have himself or be able to give his sisters. He looked and felt like a man very contented with his lot and they deserved some sated contentment before she told him exactly who she was and what she had sitting in Government Bonds waiting for her to decide what to do with it.

'I expect your mother was terrified,' she said as she snuggled deeper into his arms with a feeling of rich promise for the future and a few aches at the heart of her she had never expected to feel with him after he had turned away from her that night in Mrs Corham's garden. Both of them had remade their futures tonight, but she did not want to undo a single second of the new life ahead of them.

Chapter Sixteen

Darius fought sleep and a dreamy sense of contentment as he felt his own particular governess let go of
her acute senses in his arms. One moment she was
staring up at him as if she adored him a lot more than
he had ever dared to hope she might and the next she
was sound asleep and snuggling into his shoulder as
if she could not bear to part from him in sleep either.

Worn out, he had to suppose and smiled a cocky
smile at the glowing fire as he recalled exactly why
Miss Felicity Grantham was so spent and content to
sleep in his arms like a well-fed cat—as if she had
handed over all her responsibilities to him for the night
and knew he would guard her like a knight of old.

She was as curvaceous and perfect and sensu-
ously responsive almost next to his skin as he had
dreamt of her being night after night in his empty
and ancient bed at Owlet Manor ever since the day
they met. He had never had a lover like her, never
felt as sated and content and…

Let's face it, Darius, just plain randy.

As he felt again already, with her snuggled against him and his cock as eager for her as if they had never satisfied each other so extravagantly only a few moments ago. Well, it would have to wait; she was an ex-virgin tonight and she had walked far too far before they got here soaking wet and marooned from the world for the night. He was fiercely relieved they had been with hindsight. Guiltily delighted that she would have to marry him now and share his struggle to get the house and farms back on the road to security and profit.

His reminiscent grin turned into a frown as he recalled exactly what he had tied her to with his inability to resist her glorious body and brave spirit. They would have to wed after tonight anyway, so they might as well have made it worth their while. And it was worth it, every last gasp and murmur and the deep, deep satisfaction of making love to her. They would make a good life together, him and his own particular governess.

He watched her sleep and smiled a reminiscent smile. She was not going to be a placid and compliant wife, he decided, and looked forward to meeting Mrs Felicity Yelverton with a bone-deep certainty he was going to be a very happy man whether he deserved to be or not. He did not deserve the astonishing good luck of being forced by circumstances to wed the one woman he had ever met whom he really wanted to marry. If not for his sisters, he would be blissfully happy to hold her sleeping after making love to her with every finesse and ounce of willpower he had in him to make it special for her as well as him.

Marianne might be right; maybe she had had her one great chance at love and marriage and took it eagerly and with her eyes wide open. But Viola was governess to the wards of a man Darius would not trust within a mile of his little sister if he had any choice about the matter. When he had come back from France to the news that Viola had accepted a position as governess to Sir Harry Marbeck's late cousin's orphaned children he was within a hair's breadth of riding to Chantry Old Hall and calling the cynical devil out. At least she was not living there, under the same roof as a notorious rake and ne'er-do-well. Marianne had managed to shout her way past the red mist of rage and fear he had for his little sister. It was only when she told him that Viola was living two miles from the place in the home the children had once shared with their parents, chaperoned by an impeccably upright maiden aunt of the children's late mother, that he reluctantly abandoned his plan to rip Sir Harry limb from limb and feed him to the fish in his own lake. He decided the man could live if he really had to and hoped his unexpected inheritance would mean Viola had no need to work for her living ever again.

Yet another disappointment, he brooded as his own precious governess slept the sleep of an innocent heart in his arms. So he had planned to wed a fortune until Felicity the argumentative and delicious and just plain irresistible walked into his life. So what was he going to do now? Marry her, of course, but what about Viola and Marianne? Fortune hunting was clearly impossible now and murdering the drawling fop endangering his little sister's reputation was not a viable solution now he had even more reason not to want to be executed for it. He supposed he would just have to do what he had done for the last few years and hope his sisters were as good at looking after themselves as they had always insisted they were. That was it then, problem laid aside as unsolvable and his fate safely in his arms and blissfully asleep. His life might be a little bit uncomfortable at the edges here and there until Owlet Manor was back in profit, but overall it looked very sweet indeed. He might as well doze his way through the abating storm outside and perhaps even a little bit into the day until his lady stirred and they could be up and about the rest of their lives again, but this time together.

'Breakfast,' Fliss said, surprised how hungry she was after a night of passion. 'Hmm, these apples are a bit wrinkled, but a good choice to carry in a pack. And here are some dates and even an orange although I am not sure what we are supposed to crack the nuts with.'

'A stone, I suppose,' Darius said and grinned as

he bashed a walnut with a handy one and chewed on one half-kernel as he handed her the other.

'Tea would have been nice,' she said wistfully.

'Or coffee,' he argued and she could see breakfasts with both and a hearty helping of whatever he usually had to eat stretching ahead of them down the years as she sipped her tea and he downed his coffee and Marianne ate whatever she wanted to before the toil of the day began again.

'We have water, though.'

'And oranges,' he replied with a boyish grin as he finished peeling one and passed the segments to her.

'Share,' she demanded with a firm nod to tell him she was not a pet to be fed titbits from the breakfast table, always supposing they had a table.

'Always,' he promised and how she wished they did not have to have that talk about her fortune she had been avoiding ever since they woke up to a hazy but dry morning and a newly remade world for Darius and Fliss. She was going to be Mrs Yelverton— the sound of it even inside her own head felt so right she squirmed with delight and smiled up at him like a besotted wife, or lover. She really wanted to stay here and seduce him into making love to her all over again, but there was Juno still to find and a wedding to arrange and he might not even want to make love to her again once she had told him all her secrets.

As soon as they had eaten and tidied the hut and left it as neat as they could for the next people who needed it, they had to put on their wet shoes and leave. It felt more urgent to get back to Broadley and reality whenever she remembered Juno was out there somewhere and might be soaking wet and still walking to Broadley.

They carefully made their way down the still-muddy path and it seemed such a short walk in full daylight and without the driving rain of last night. She reached the place where the path broadened almost into a proper lane and turned to try to catch a last glimpse of their rough shelter, but it was already out of sight. Was it sentimental of her to wish they could come up here now and again over the years and renew the wonder of their first love making in the rough shelter of its walls while summer rain tumbled down outside and they made their own luxury of loving inside it?

'Do you think she is safe?' she asked as painful anxiety overtook the lovely, lingering afterglow of that loving and reminded her why they had been up here in the first place.

'I am very nearly sure of it, since she has spent the last few years with you and some of your cleverness must have rubbed off on her along the way.'

'Thank you. I am not sure you will think me quite so clever when you find out what I have—'

Fliss let her words die away as her mouth fell open in shock. She stared at the tall and powerful figure of Lord Stratford striding towards them through mud, puddles and wet grass. It was only just after dawn and the Viscount looked as if he had been up all night. He was mud splashed and unshaven as if he had ridden straight to Miss Donne's and never mind the state he was in. She had never seen him even slightly unkempt before, nor furiously angry. There was a frown like thunder on his usually coolly composed face as he loped towards them at the double.

'I am going to kill you and feed your liver to the vultures,' he informed Darius through gritted teeth.

'I doubt it,' Darius replied with his best Captain Yelverton look of superiority and Lord Stratford actually raised his fists so she stepped between them.

With the glow of their loving still inside her to say he probably had some reason to be angry, she supposed it was obvious to a man of Lord Stratford's intelligence and experience that she and Darius had made glorious love to one another last night while they were stuck up on the hill listening to the pouring rain.

'Don't be ridiculous, Your Lordship,' his Felicity told the very angry man glaring at Darius as if he could read every lusty thought in his head about this wondrous woman he was about to marry and apparently this furious stranger did not like a single one of them. 'There are no vultures in this country,' she added sternly and Darius felt a little less flattered that she had sprung to his defence.

'I will import some especially,' the dark and dangerous-looking aristocrat in his beautifully cut boots and coat and riding breeches that looked as if they might have been slept in said without even breaking his stride. 'There is still enough ice left in my icehouse to store him on until they arrive. I will just have to hope they are very hungry after their long journey.'

Fliss remained stubbornly in front of Darius despite her academic argument with the other man. He clicked his tongue impatiently and tried to step around her, but she dodged in front of him every time he moved so he felt even more ridiculous and stood still again.

'Hiding behind a petticoat, are you? You are a worm, sir. I demand you meet me if you lack the courage to come out from behind Miss Grantham's skirts and face me like a man,' the stranger goaded him with a lordly sneer.

'I would if I could,' Darius said as he tried to dodge around his over-protective wife-to-be yet again and just ended up feeling even more stupid.

'Don't be so foolish, my lord. His sister tells me Darius was considered to be the finest marksman in his regiment and I really do not want you to shoot him anyway since I am going to marry him.'

'Are you indeed?' Lord Whoever-He-Was barked as if that piece of news had only added fuel to the already scorching heat of his fury. 'We will soon see about that.'

'No, we will not,' Fliss said very firmly indeed.

Darius had to admire her stern lack of respect for

a title, even if he wanted to mill the stranger down and get on with his day, Lord or not. He had a runaway girl still to find and a wedding to arrange; he was a busy man and this stranger was confoundedly in the way.

'I have come to a decision about the future at last,' Fliss shocked him by telling the man as if he had a right to know. 'And I have decided I cannot enter a marriage of convenience with you, my lord, since I fully intend making one of inconvenience with the man I love instead.'

'Do you indeed?' the man enquired so coldly at least Fliss was right about it only ever being a convenient idea between them because there was no sign of any emotion in the man's eyes but bad temper and a pinch of frustrated pride.

Darius allowed he might have a reason for all that aristocratic anger if he had made Fliss an offer of marriage she must have been undecided about accepting, or he would never have met her in the first place. Or he would have been too late when he did so that day in the woods and that idea seemed unthinkable.

'Yes,' she said, her enchantingly firm chin raised and a defiant glare for both of them, just in case they decided to ignore her and fight anyway. 'I very definitely do,' she added and that was a relief, wasn't it?

Darius knew the bottom would drop out of his world if she had weighed them both in the balance and decided she would rather like a title and whatever

riches came with it after all. Did he love her then?
Probably. No, he did love her. With every last idi-
otic thought in his stupid head and every cell in his
body he adored her and would do so until his dying
day—even if she had been considering marriages
of convenience with arrogant lords while his back
was turned and that would definitely have to stop.

'Good,' he said as it was the only word he had
right now and he meant it so deeply he only hoped
she knew he was desperate to march up the aisle to
her and say yes to the future. Felicity soon-to-be Yelverton was the love of his life.

'Who are you then, *Darius*?' His Lordship demanded rudely.

If the man was not so confoundedly in the way
he could almost pity him for losing the place he had
wanted to take in Fliss's life. The place where he belonged, he recalled more fiercely and glared at the
stranger again. 'Darius Yelverton of Owlet Manor,
which I judge to be about seven miles away from
here as the crow flies and on the other side of Broadley from where we are now. Are *you* the idiot who
has been trying to force Miss Grantham's former
pupil to wed an old man against her will?'

'No, that particular idiot is my mother,' Lord
Whichever-He-Was snapped impatiently and Darius decided he might have liked him in different circumstances, if the man had not wanted to marry his
own future wife, of course.

'Then where were you when the girl needed you?'

he asked abruptly and this time Fliss frowned at him instead of her lordly suitor and ex-employer.

'France,' the man said with what looked like a squirm of guilt, despite that air of impatient superiority that made Darius's fists itch to thump him.

'Lord Stratford is a diplomat,' Fliss explained hastily, obviously wondering if she needed to step between them again.

'Really?' Darius drawled. No doubt the man handed out compliments to visiting princesses very handily, but he seemed as diplomatic as an angry bull right now. They were so absorbed in glaring at one another it was not until she was nearly on them that Darius realised his sister was striding towards them with a militant look on her face.

'Thank goodness you are both safe,' Marianne said abruptly.

'Not you again,' Lord Stratford snapped disgustedly, as if he had already met her and had not relished the meeting one bit.

Darius saw his sister stiffen, then glare at the man as if she would be willing to meet him with pistols at dawn even if Darius had been going off the idea until she turned up to be glowered at by the nobility.

'Oh, be quiet—all of you,' Fliss said and of course she wanted an answer to the most important question of all—how could he have forgotten it? 'Is Juno safe and well?' she asked with all of last night's painful guilt and anxiety in her darkest of blue eyes—of course, that was the colour of them, he realised, and knew he had the ultimate intimacy of being her lover to thank for knowing that lovely detail of her at long last as he stared down at her with every right to do so now he knew how much he loved her.

'Well, she was seen early this morning,' Marianne said cautiously and with a sidelong glare at Lord Stratford.

'Where and what is being done about it?' the man demanded as if he would like to wring an answer out of her.

'He arrived early this morning and has been reorganising the search for Miss Defford ever since, Fliss. I suppose Lord Stratford is intent on dragging the poor girl back to London so he can make her marry that old man,' Marianne challenged him contemptuously.

'Of course I am not,' he snapped, looking revolted by the very idea. 'Now tell me where my ward is and if she is being properly looked after. Is she soaked to the skin after last night's storm? Has she taken a chill or a fever?'

'How do you expect me to believe you care when you neglected the poor girl so shockingly? No wonder she ran away rather than wed some old man with a title.'

'Damn fool idea,' he mumbled as if he thought so, too. Darius felt some sympathy with him even if he was Fliss's rejected suitor. 'I am the one who needs to marry, so that my wife can look after Juno instead of my mother,' the lordly fool blurted out and he must be even more tired than he looked to have spoken his private business out loud, but Darius withdrew his fellow feeling since Fliss was the bride he had had in mind for that position. As if the idiot could simply employ her as his wife rather than his ward's governess when that position became redundant.

'Where was Juno last seen then, Marianne?' Fliss pleaded for the information. For a moment Marianne looked suspicious of the Lord in their midst, then gave in.

'It's the oddest thing, Fliss. Apparently a dark-haired girl of medium height and slender build was seen on the Leominster road not long after dawn. We were all so sure she was heading towards Broadley in order to find you that we did not even bother to search that way until a carter came forward to say he had seen her walking away from the town this morning instead of towards it.'

'Why on earth would she do such a thing?' Fliss said.

Darius saw how much her shoulders had slumped and sensed how hard it was for her to hear such a peculiar piece of news. 'Did he say if she seemed well and whether she was wet from yesterday's rain?' he asked.

'He only had a fleeting glimpse before she turned away from the road as if she did not want to be seen, but he said she could move easily and her clothes did not look sodden or dragging her back as they would if she had been out in the storm all last night.'

'Thank heavens for that, then,' Fliss said and Lord Stratford nodded and turned to walk down the hill as if he had all but forgotten the rest of them.

'He's right,' Marianne said rather surprisingly after her prickly dislike of the man had seemed so obvious at her first glare at his unshaven face just now. 'We can quarrel later; after we have found Miss Defford.'

'True,' Darius agreed with a nod and Fliss shook her head at both of them as they set out to follow the impatient Lord Stratford down the hill to Broadley.

Chapter Seventeen

'Are you are a fortune hunter?' Lord Stratford asked Darius when they had finally caught up with him just before the first cottages of the town were in view.

With his arm around her waist to make sure she did not slip on the still-muddy path, and because he wanted it there and never mind the path, Darius felt Fliss wince at that baffling question. 'Of course not,' she said for him.

'Why would I compromise Miss Grantham for the sake of a fortune she does not have?' he asked, puzzled by the tension he could feel in her body and the odd look Lord Stratford was giving him as if he almost pitied him.

'You don't have one of those, do you?' he almost joked as he looked into her eyes and saw another anxiety there.

'I do, actually,' she said so airily he knew she

was worried about his reaction to that startling piece of news.

'You do?'

'Yes, I do.'

Darius sensed dangerous ground under his feet as dratted Lord Stratford looked on with a faintly ironic smile. He was not having the love of his life whisked away by some self-satisfied aristocrat because she had more money than he thought. 'Good,' he said with a bland smile.

'Good?' she echoed as if she could hardly believe her ears.

'We will not have to be poor, so why would it not be good? How rich are you?'

'I inherited thirty thousand pounds three months ago,' she said.

His Lordship looked faintly offended by their open discussion of her money and Darius recalled it simply was not good *ton* to discuss it in public. So the man ought to take himself off and leave them to it if he did not want to be offended.

'And you never thought to tell me?' he asked her mildly.

'No,' she said starkly and his fortune-hunting plans felt raw between them for a heavy moment.

'At least you can be comfortable in my ramshackle old house while I make enough money to keep you and whatever family we may have in the future, then.'

'And you can make the improvement on the farms that you are so desperate to put in hand.'

'It is just as well I love you, though,' he said in front of her rejected suitor and his own sister, because he had gone beyond embarrassment now and this felt too important for them to be polite and reserved about until they had the chance to say it all in private.

'Luckily I had already managed to work that out for myself,' she said.

'And…?' he said encouragingly.

'And I am surprised you even have to ask.'

'Nevertheless I do still have to ask if you think you could ever love me back.'

'Of course I love you, you great blind fool.'

'Oh, good,' the Lord said in such a sarcastic tone of voice Darius began to wonder about hitting him after all.

'I thought you came here to worry about your ward, Lord Stratford,' his sister said so coolly even Darius shivered.

'I did,' he said and with one last disgusted look at the three of them he strode off down the hill again as if they were best forgotten.

'Trust me to make sure he sends the right people in the right direction and Miss Donne will probably manage to make him take a bath and shave when he gets there, so he will be less weary and irritable with the rest of the searchers than he was with you. You two can safely leave the rest of us to find Miss

Defford now while you get your future sorted out,'
Marianne told them sternly. 'He is Juno Defford's
guardian, after all, so she is his responsibility and
he will be the one with every right to be stamping
about the countryside giving orders now he has finally turned up to take responsibility for her,' she
added, then dashed on down the hill in the wake of
the tall Lord's currently rather scruffy figure.

'And she thinks we need time to settle our differences,' Darius told Fliss.

'Do we?' she asked half-seriously.

'No, you say you love me and you have fogged
my brain and done drastic things to the rest of me
from the first moment I laid eyes on you. I could almost like that Stratford fellow for not being sharp
enough to persuade you to marry him before he left
for France. He might have married you before he
went and what a terrible idea that is.'

'Since I had a say in whether he did or not, I
rather doubt it. I was very torn about the idea until
you rejected me that night in Mrs Corham's garden.
After that I thought I might as well marry him for
convenience, since I was clearly not going to do it
for love with you.'

'Fool.'

'You or me?'

'Both of us from the sound of things and you
are not keeping any more dark secrets from me, are

you?' he asked as they moved closer until his arm was about her waist and who cared who saw them now? He certainly did not and she looked quite happy to stroll along the lane into Broadley like this when anyone might see them arm in arm and draw their own conclusions.

'No,' she said after a short pause as if she was examining her conscience. 'Apart from the fact my unloving uncle is the Earl of Netherton. That is not a secret, but I try not to talk about him or the rest of my mother's family any more than I must.'

'I hope he does not expect your future husband to beg his consent for our marriage, then. He must be the uncle who put you out in the world to make your own living at seventeen and I will not forgive him for that in a hurry even if you manage to one day.'

'We would never have met if he had taken me to London and found me a quietly respectable husband instead,' she pointed out.

'I hope I am not too much of a disappointment for you then,' he said half-seriously, because he was far less of a catch than her Viscount, even if they were going to be richer than he had thought they would be between them.

'No, you are my reward for being good all these years.'

'We were not very good last night.'

'Now I thought we were very good indeed,' she said with a wicked smile he hoped he was about to get very used to and on a daily basis.

'Oh, we were, but unfortunately we will have to be virtuous again until we can obtain a special licence and get married, or at least we will if I am any judge of your Miss Donne's determination to keep us respectable for the next few weeks.'

'Aye, you are right, she will be eager to see all is perfectly proper between us from now on until our wedding night, especially after such a disgraceful lapse last night.'

'Just as well your lordly uncle does not care what you do as long as you don't do it at his expense, love, or I might find myself on the wrong end of his horsewhip.'

'You still might find yourself on that end of Lord Stratford's if you go about kissing me in the street,' she said with a provocative little wriggle against his over-eager body to make sure he followed that half-formed intention through, with interest. His intimate, eager interest and the curiosity of a couple of villagers clearly setting out on their day before the rest of the townsfolk were stirring.

'Why would he care?' he said jealously as soon as he could find the willpower to stop making love to his future wife in public.

'Because I was Juno's governess and he is feeling guilty that he put his duty to his country before his duty to her, so he might decide my conduct reflects on his ward's reputation. Particularly when he will find it very difficult indeed to hide the fact she ran away from his mother's ridiculous attempt to marry her off behind his back.'

'He should feel guilty about her,' he said, then shook his head. 'As if I have any right to judge when I put my duty before my own sister's happiness. I should have sold out and come home with Marianne after Badajoz.'

'As if that would have helped her,' Fliss said and smoothed a loving finger over the heavy frown knitting his brows until he relaxed and wondered if she could be right.

'I suppose you think me an overprotective fool.'

'Only part of the time,' she teased him with a fleeting kiss on the cheek, then unwound their touch until they were only holding hands and less than that was impossible for both of them this morning while they made their slow way back to Miss Donne's without much idea of how the rest of the world felt about seeing them dishevelled and love lost so scandalously early in the day.

'I still worry about Viola working for such a scoundrel,' he said a little bit sheepishly as the idea he might have to let both his sisters live their lives the way they chose to began to sink in under Fliss's sceptical gaze.

'And Marianne, does she work for one, too?' she asked with a roguish smile he must add to his catalogue of reasons why he was not going to let her out of his bed for long once he finally got his wife in it and all that lusty legal loving to look forward to. 'I am relying on you to convince her she must stay with us after we are wed, by the way,' she added as if she already knew his sister's fierce streak of independence too well.

Marianne would try to leave them on the pretext she was in the way, she was quite right. 'Now that really will have to be a joint enterprise,' he said. 'My sister is not easily persuaded once she has made up her mind.'

'I like the sound of a joint enterprise. I want to be an active and involved farmer's wife, Darius. Promise you will not cut me out of your life and make me feel like a ladylike decoration for Owlet Manor.'

'I can safely promise you that. I was dreading you might insist I turn into a proper gentleman and lord of the manor instead of working my own land with the men whenever necessary and I would be bored in a sennight.'

'So there you are, you see? We are perfectly suited because I would be if you wanted me to be a proper lady.'

'That we are, my love, that we are,' he told her with all the love and promise their future held in his heart as he looked down at her.

Never mind that they seemed to have reached Miss Donne's doorstep without noticing how they got here, he kissed her with all the passion and wonder of finding love despite his worst efforts and to the devil with anyone who might be nosy enough to be watching them. She put her arms about his neck and tugged him even closer, so they were locked in one another's arms as if they might make love in the open when the lady of the house opened her back door and caught them in time.

'Hmm, luckily Marianne warned me what to expect when you finally got here, but the sooner we get you two married and safely tucked away at Owlet Manor where you will only be able to shock her and the sheep, the better,' that lady said with the biggest, most triumphant smile Darius had ever seen on such a respectable spinster lady's face.

'It cannot be too soon for me,' he told Fliss's true family with a rueful grin.

'Me neither,' Fliss said and her smile was like the sun coming out on this cloud-hazed July morning. With so many things still to do they exchanged a guilty look before they entered Miss Donne's cottage hand in hand. 'I do love you, Darius Yelverton.'

'And I love you, my Felicity. And that is what you are, so I might have to get attached to your full name after all.'

'Just promise me you will not insist on naming our daughter with it and I will be happy.'

'I will be happy just to have you safe and her as well and never mind the name whenever she chooses to arrive, my love,' he murmured and kissed her full on the lips in front of Miss Donne and the gaping kitchen maid.

'Who would have thought it,' the girl said, 'what

with her being a proper lady and him supposed to a soldier and a gentleman?'

'Who indeed?' Miss Donne said with a smug smile and bustled them both out of the room so Fliss and Darius could kiss each other witless in peace.

* * * * *

If you enjoyed this book, why not check out these other great reads by Elizabeth Beacon

The Governess Heiress
A Wedding for the Scandalous Heiress
A Rake to the Rescue
The Duchess's Secret

And look out for more books in The Yelverton Marriages series, coming soon!